Danish Fairy Tales

Danish Fairy Tales

SVENDT GRUNDTVIG

TRANSLATED BY J. GRANT CRAMER

ILLUSTRATED BY
DREW VAN HEUSEN

DOVER PUBLICATIONS, INC.
NEW YORK

Published in Canada by General Publishing Company, Ltd.,
30 Lesmill Road, Don Mills, Toronto, Ontario.
Published in the United Kingdom by Constable and
Company, Ltd., 10 Orange Street, London WC 2.

This Dover edition, first published in 1972, is an unabridged
republication of the work as published in 1919 by the Four
Seas Company. The illustrations were made for the Dover
edition by Drew van Heusen.

International Standard Book Number: 0-486-22891-6
Library of Congress Catalog Card Number: 72-91057

Manufactured in the United States of America
Dover Publications, Inc.
180 Varick Street
New York, N.Y. 10014

Preface

These Danish folk-tales, and many more, were originally collected by Svendt Grundtvig, a Danish professor and philologist, (1824-1883). He found that throughout all the country districts, men and women were telling stories and reciting ballads that they had learned from their grandmothers, who, in their turn, had heard them from crooners of old songs, and tellers of old tales. Professor Grundtvig realized that these echoes of an earlier time were precious; that, if they were not perpetuated in written form, they would be lost. It was a labor of love on his part to collect these tales; a labor that lasted over twenty years, and that enlisted the aid of many of his countrymen. Grundtvig says that he has kept the simplicity and artlessness of the oral tradition; and that, in the case of varying versions from different parts of the country, he has taken the purer and more complete form, but has always preserved the epic unity.

The translator of these tales spent a part of his boyhood in Denmark, where his father was United States Minister. There he heard many of these stories, which were told him by a man-servant who came from Jutland. Jensen had not read any of these tales; but they, with many others, were stored in his memory. He had always known them, he said.

In these Danish stories we have the familiar situations that we find in folk-tales from widely different sources: the transformation of human beings into beings of a lower order, the far journeys, the wicked stepmother, the impossible tasks, the magic birth, the mysterious commands, the violation of which brings doom upon the unfortunate mortal, the usual discomfiture of the wicked and triumph of the good.

There are, naturally, these stock features. But there is something rarer that stamps these tales with an originality that seems to individualize them. This quality, may, perhaps, be found in the tenderness and poetic atmosphere of the Green Knight; in the naivete of Peter Ox and the pessimistic moralizing of Good Deeds; in the humorous expression of the very human satisfaction of outwitting another, in The Treasure; as well as in the charm of The Pleiades, with its quaint naming, or rather, no-naming of the sons, and with its beautiful ending. One may even imagine here a happy linking of their fairyland wonders with those of our own day. For the ship that can go over land and sea, that can propel itself, does it not suggest our modern wonder, the motor, that controls not only land and water, but sky as well? And the power to hear in one country what is being said in another, does it not suggest the telephone, or the greater marvel of wireless telegraphy?

Today we know the wizard, and name him electricity. We do not know him altogether; there is more wizardry to come. But there will be no more folk-tales; they have all been told. The people who first told them lived very long ago, and did not understand the world around them. To the child, Nature is personal; the wind is his "unseen playmate." Our primitive ancestor, too, was a child. The wind was personal to him also; but a magic force controlled it, a wizard, perhaps, who could use his mighty power to work one harm. And so, the sun, as it sank into the sea, and the seasons which came and went, suggested conflict, or enmity, or enchantment on the part of one power, and final triumph on the part of the other. Accordingly, we find in their stories transformations, enchantments, and magic deliverances. But these were really no more wonderful than the miracle of nature which was passing before their uncomprehending eyes.

M.N.C.

Contents

The Pleiades

There was once a man and he had six sons. He did not give them, however, any names such as other people have, but called them according to their age, the Oldest, Next to the Oldest, the Next to the Next to the Oldest, the Next to the Next to the Youngest, the Next to the Youngest and the Youngest. They had no other names.

When the Oldest was eighteen and the Youngest twelve, their father sent them out into the world that each might learn a trade. They went together for a short distance until they came to a place where six roads diverged; there they separated and each was to go his own way. But before parting they agreed to meet in two years at that same place and to return to their father together.

On the day appointed they all met and went home to their father who asked each one what he had learned. The Oldest said that he was a ship-builder and could build ships which could propel themselves. The Next to the Oldest had gone to sea and had become a helmsman and could steer a ship over land as well as over water. The Next to the Next to the Oldest had only learned to listen, but that he could do so well that when he was in one country he could hear what was going on in another. The Next to the Next to the Youngest had become a sharpshooter, and he never missed his aim. The Next to the Youngest had learned how to climb, and he could climb up a wall like a fly and no cliff was too steep for him to scale.

When the father had heard what the five brothers could do, he said that it was all very well but that he had expected something more from them. Then he asked what the Youngest had learned; he had great hopes in him for he was his favorite. The Youngest was glad that it was at last his turn to speak, and he answered joyously that he had become a master-thief. When his father heard that, he was furious and exclaimed, "Shame on you, for the disgrace that you have brought upon me and the whole family."

Now it happened that at this very time the king's beautiful young daughter had been stolen by a wicked wizard, and the king promised the half of his realm and the princess in marriage to the one who should free her from the wizard. When the six brothers heard this they resolved to try their luck. The shipbuilder built a ship that went of itself. The helmsman steered it over land and sea. The listener listened carefully and at last said that he heard the wizard inside a mountain of glass. Thither they sailed. The climber quickly climbed to the top of the mountain and saw the ugly wizard lying sleeping with his head in the lap of the princess. Then he hurried down, and taking the little master-thief on his back, went into the inside of the mountain. The thief stole the princess so cleverly from under the head of the wizard that he did not notice it, but continued to sleep.

As soon as they were on board, the ship sailed away, but the listener had to continue to keep a watch on the wizard. When they were not far from land he said to the others: "Now the wizard is awaking! now he is stretching himself! now he misses the princess! now he is coming!"

Now the king's daughter was beside herself with fear, and declared that they would all die if there were not a sharpshooter on board. The wizard could fly throught the air and would soon overtake them; he was also invulnerable except in one small black spot, not larger than a pinhead, in the middle of his chest. Hardly had she finished speaking when they saw the wizard in the distance rushing through the air. The sharpshooter took careful aim, shot, and his bullet struck the little black spot and at once the wizard burst into thousands of fiery pieces, and these we know as meteorites.

At last the six brothers reached home with the princess and brought her to the king. But they were all in love with her, and each one could truthfully say that without his help she could not have been saved. Then the king was distressed, for he did not know to whom he should give his daughter. And the princess was also sad, for she did not know whom she loved best.

But God would not that there should be strife among them, so he sent death to the six brothers and to the king's daughter in one and the same night. Then he made of the seven a constellation which men call the Pleiades. And of these stars the brightest is the princess and the faintest the little master-thief.

Peter Ox

There were once upon a time a peasant and his wife who lived in Jutland, but they had no children. They often lamented that fact and were also sad to think that they had no relatives to whom to leave their farm and other possessions. So the years went by and they became richer and richer, but there was no one to inherit their wealth.

One year the farmer bought a fine calf which he called Peter, and it was really the finest animal that he had ever seen, and so clever that it seemed to understand nearly everything that one said to it. It was also very amusing and affectionate, so that the man and his wife soon became as fond of it as if it were their own child.

One day the farmer said to his wife, "Perhaps the sexton of our church could teach Peter to talk; then we could not do better than to adopt him as our child, and he could then inherit all our property."

"Who can tell?" said the wife, "Our sexton is a learned man and perhaps he might be able to teach Peter to talk, for Peter is really very clever. Suppose you ask the sexton."

So the farmer went over to the sexton and asked him whether he did not believe that he could teach his calf to talk, because he wanted to make the animal his heir. The crafty sexton looked around to see that no one was near, and then said that he thought he could do so. "Only you must not tell anybody," he said, "for it must be a great secret, and the minister in particular must not know anything about it, or I might get into serious trouble as such things are strictly forbidden. Moreover it will cost a pretty penny as we shall need rare and expensive books." The farmer said that he did not mind, and handing the sexton a hundred dollars to buy books with, promised not to say a word about the arrangement to anyone.

That evening the man brought his calf to the sexton who promised to do his best. In about a week the farmer returned to see how his calf was getting on, but the sexton said that he did not dare let him see the animal, else Peter might become homesick and forget all that he had already learned. Otherwise he was making good progress, but the farmer must pay another hundred dollars, as Peter needed more books. The peasant happened to have the money with him, so he gave it to the sexton and went home filled with hope and pleasant anticipations.

At the end of another week the man again went to make inquiry about Peter, and was told by the sexton that he was doing fairly well. "Can he say anything?" asked the farmer.

"Yes, he can say 'Ma,' " answered the sexton.

"The poor animal is surely ill," said the peasant, "and he probably wants mead. I will go straight home and bring him a jug of it." So he fetched a jug of good, old mead and gave it to the sexton for Peter. The sexton, however, kept the mead and gave the calf some milk instead.

A week later the farmer came again to find out what Peter could say now. "He still refuses to say anything but 'Ma,' " said the sexton.

"Oh! he is a cunning rogue;" said the peasant, "so he wants more mead, does he? Well, I'll get him some more, as he likes it so much. But what progress has he made?"

"He is doing so well," answered the sexton, "that he needs another hundred dollars' worth of books, for he cannot learn anything more from those that he has now."

"Well then, if he needs them he shall have them." So that same day the farmer brought another hundred dollars and a jug of good, old mead for Peter.

Now the peasant allowed a few weeks to elapse without calling on Peter, for he began to be afraid that each visit would cost him a hundred dollars. In the meantime the calf had become as fat as he would ever be, so the sexton killed him and sold the meat carefully at a distance from the village. Having done that he put on his black clothes and went to call on the farmer and his wife. As soon as he had bid them good day he asked them whether Peter had reached home safe and sound.

"Why no," said the farmer, "he has not run away, has he?"

"I hope," said the sexton, "that after all the trouble I have taken he has not been so tricky as to run away and to abuse my confidence so shamefully. For I have spent at least a hundred dollars of my own money to pay for books for him. Now Peter could say whatever he wanted, and he was telling me only yesterday that he was longing to see his dear parents. As I wanted to give him that pleasure, but feared that he would not be able to find his way home alone, I dressed myself and started out with him. We were hardly in the street when I suddenly remembered that I had left my stick at home, so I ran back to get it. When I came out of the house again, I found that Peter had run on alone. I thought, of course, that he had gone back to your house. If he is not there I certainly do not know where he can be."

Then the people began to weep and lament that Peter was lost, now especially when they might have had such pleasure with him, and after paying out so much money for his education. And the worst of it was that they were again without an heir. The sexton tried to comfort them and was also very sorry that Peter had deceived them so. But perhaps he had only lost his way, and the sexton promised that he would ask publicly in church next Sunday whether somebody had not seen the calf. Then he bade the farmer and his wife goodbye and went home and had some good roast veal for dinner.

One day the sexton read in the paper that a new merchant, named Peter Ox, had settled in the neighboring town. He put the paper into his pocket and went straight to the farmer and read this item of news to him. "One might almost believe," he said, "that this is your calf."

"Why yes," said the farmer, "who else should it be?" Then his wife added, "Yes father, go at once to see him, for I feel sure that it can be no other than our dear Peter. But take along plenty of money for he probably needs it now that he has become a merchant."

On the following morning the farmer put a bag of money on his shoulder, took with him some provisions, and started to walk to the town where the merchant lived. Early next morning he arrived there and went straight to the merchant's house. The servants told the man that the merchant had not gotten up yet. "That does not make any difference for I am his father; just take me up to his room."

So they took the peasant up to the bedroom where the merchant lay sound asleep. And as soon as the farmer saw him, he recognized Peter. There were the same thick neck and broad forehead and the same red hair, but otherwise he looked just like a human being. Then the man went to him and bade him good morning and said, "Well, Peter, you caused your mother and me great sorrow when you ran away as soon as you had learned something. But get up now and let me have a look at you and talk with you."

The merchant, of course, believed that he had a crazy man to deal with, so he thought it best to be careful. "Yes I will get up," he said, and jumped out of bed into his clothes as quickly as possible.

"Ah!" said the peasant, "now I see what a wise man our sexton was; he has brought it to pass that you are like any other man. If I were not absolutely certain of it, I should never dream that you were the calf of our red cow. Will you come home with me?" The merchant said that he could not as he had to attend to his business. "But you could take over my farm and I would retire. Nevertheless if you prefer to stay in business, I am willing. Do you need any money?"

"Well," said the merchant, "a man can always find use for money in his business."

"I thought so," said the farmer, "and besides you had nothing to start with, so I have brought you some money." And with that he poured out on the table the bright dollars that covered it entirely.

When the merchant saw what kind of a man his new found acquaintance was, he chatted with him in a very friendly manner and begged him to remain with him for a few days.

"Yes indeed," said the farmer, "but you must be sure to call me father from now on."

"But I have neither father nor mother living," answered Peter Ox.

"That I know perfectly well," the peasant replied, "for I sold your real father in Copenhagen last Michaelmas, and your mother died while calving. But my wife and I have adopted you as our child and you will be our heir, so you must call me father."

The merchant gladly agreed to that and kept the bag of money; and before leaving town the farmer made his will and bequeathed all his possessions to Peter after his death. Then the man went home and told his wife the whole story, and she was delighted to learn that the merchant Peter Ox was really their own calf.

"Now you must go straight over to the sexton and tell him what has happened;" she said, "and be sure to refund to him the hundred dollars that he paid out of his own pocket for Peter, for he has earned all that we have paid him, because of the joy that he has caused us in giving us such a son and heir."

Her husband was of the same opinion and went to call on the sexton, whom he thanked many times for his kindness and to whom he also gave two hundred dollars.

Then the farmer sold his farm, and he and his wife moved into the town where the merchant was, and lived with him happily until their death.

The Green
Knight

Drew van Seusen

Once upon a time there were a king and a queen and they had but one little daughter, and when she was very young her dear mother became sick unto death. When the queen knew that she had only a short time to live, she called the king and said, "My dear lord and husband! in order that I may die in peace you must promise me one thing, and that is, that you will never refuse our child anything that she may ask of you if it be possible to grant her wish." That the king promised her and she died soon afterward.

The king's heart was nearly broken for he loved his wife devotedly, and his little daughter alone could comfort him. The princess grew up, and the fulfilment of the promise was indeed easy for the king; he never refused her a request. That spoiled her a little, but otherwise she was a dear, good child who only needed a mother to understand and love her; for the lack of this she was often moody and melancholy. The princess did not care for games and amusements like other children, but instead she liked to wander alone in the gardens and woods, and above all she loved flowers and birds and animals, and she was also fond of reading poetry and stories.

Not far from the palace there lived the widow of a count, who had a daughter a little older than the princess. The young countess, however, was not a good girl, but was vain, selfish and hard-hearted; on the other hand she was clever, like her mother, and could dissimulate when she thought it would serve her ends. The countess cleverly devised ways so that her daughter was often thrown together with the princess, and both mother and daughter spared no pains to please her. They did everything in their power to give her pleasure and cheer her, and soon she always had to have either one or the other by her side.

Now that was just what the countess wanted and had been working for; so that when she saw that she had brought matters to that point, she made her daughter tell the princess, amid tears, that they must now separate because she and her mother had to go far away into another country. Then the little princess ran at once to the countess and told her that she must not leave with her daughter, for she could not live without her and would grieve to death if she left her. Then the countess pretended to be deeply moved and told the princess that there was only one way that she could be persuaded to stay in the country, and that was for the king to marry her. Then both mother and daughter could always stay with her, and they painted in glowing colors the joys that would be hers if that should come to pass.

Then the princess went to her father, the king, and begged and implored him to marry the countess, for otherwise she would go away and his poor little daughter would lose her only friend and grieve to death.

"You would certainly repent of it, if I were to do it," said the king, "and I should also, for I have no desire whatever to marry, and I have no confidence in the deceitful countess and her deceitful daughter."

But the princess did not cease crying and imploring him until he promised to grant her wish. Then the king asked the countess to marry him and she at once consented. Soon after that the wedding ceremony took place and the countess became queen and was now the stepmother of the young princess.

But after the marriage all was changed. The queen did nothing but tease and torment her stepdaughter, while nothing was too good for her own child. Her daughter did not pay any attention to the poor princess, but did everything she could to make her life miserable.

The king, who could see all this, took it very much to heart, for he loved his daughter deeply; so he said to her on one occasion, "Alas, my poor little daughter, you are having a sad life and must certainly have repented many a time of that which you asked of me, for it has all turned out as I foretold. But now, unfortunately, it is too late. I think it would be better for you to leave us for a time and go out to my summer palace on the island; there you would, at least, have peace and quiet."

The princess agreed with her father, and although it was very hard for them to be separated, it was nevertheless absolutely necessary, as she could no longer endure her wicked stepmother and her malicious stepsister. So she took with her two of her ladies in waiting to live in the summer palace on the island, and her father came from time to time to visit her; and he could see very plainly that she was much happier here than she would have been at home with her wicked stepmother.

So she grew up to be a lovely maiden, pure, innocent and thoughtful, kind to both men and beasts. But she was never really happy, and there was always an undercurrent of sadness in her nature, and a longing for something better than she had hitherto found in the world.

One day her father came to her to bid her farewell, for he had to go on a long journey to be present at a gathering of kings and nobles from many lands, and would not return for a long time. The king wanted to cheer his daughter, so he said to her jestingly that he would look carefully among the princes to see whether he could not find one among them all who would be worthy to become her husband. Then the princess answered him and said: "I thank you, dear father; if you see the Green Knight, greet him and tell him that I am waiting and longing for him, for he alone and no other can free me from my suffering."

When the princess said that, she was thinking of the green churchyard with its many green mounds, for she longed for death. But the king did not understand her and wondered much at the strange greeting to a strange knight whose name he had never heard of before; but he was accustomed to grant her every wish, so he only said he would not forget to greet the knight as soon as he met him. Then he bade his daughter a tender farewell and started on his journey to the meeting of the kings.

There he found many princes, young nobles and knights, but among them there was no one called the Green Knight, so that the king could not deliver his daughter's message. At last he started on his homeward journey and had to cross high mountains and wide rivers and to go through dense forests. And as the king one day was passing through one of those great woods with his train, they came upon a large open space where thousands of boars were feeding. These were not wild, but tame, and were guarded by a swineherd in the garb of a huntsman who sat, surrounded by his dogs, on a little knoll and had a pipe to whose notes all animals listened and were obedient.

The king wondered at this herd of tame boars, and had one of his retainers ask the swineherd to whom they belonged. He answered that they belonged to the Green Knight. Then the king remembered what his daughter had asked him, and he himself rode up to the man and asked whether the Green Knight lived in the neighborhood.

"No," he replied, "he lives far from here, towards the east. If you ride in that direction you will meet other herdsmen who will show you the way to his castle."

Then the king and his men rode eastward for three days through a great forest, until they came again to a large plain surrounded by great forests, on which immense herds of elks and wild oxen were grazing. These also were guarded by a herdsman in hunter's dress, accompanied by his dogs. And the king rode to the man, who told him that all these herds belonged to the Green Knight, who lived further eastward. And again after three days the King came to a great clearing, where he saw great herds of stags and does, and the herdsman, in answer to his question, said that the Green Knight's castle was but a day's journey distant. Then the king rode for a day on green paths, through green woods, until he came to a great castle which was also green, for it was entirely covered by vines and climbing plants. When they rode up to the castle, a large number of men dressed in green like hunters, appeared and escorted them into the castle, and announced that the king of such and such a kingdom had arrived and desired to greet their master. Then the lord of the castle came himself — a tall, handsome, young man, also clad in green — and bade his guest welcome and entertained them in a lordly manner.

Then said the king: "You live far away and you have so great a domain that I had to go much out of my way to fulfill my daughter's wish. When I rode forth to attend the gathering of the kings, she asked me to greet the Green Knight for her, and to tell him how she longed for him, and that he alone could free her from her torment. This is a very strange commission that I have undertaken, but my daughter knows what is right and proper, and moreover I promised her mother on her deathbed that I would never refuse our only child a wish; so I have come here to deliver the message and keep my promise."

Then the Green Knight said to the king: "Your daughter was sad, and was certainly not thinking of me when she gave you her message, for she can never have heard of me; she was probably thinking of the churchyard with its many green mounds, where alone she hoped to find rest. But perhaps I can give her something to alleviate her sorrow. Take this little book, and tell the princess when she is sad and heavy-hearted to open her east window and to read in the book; it will gladden her heart."

Then the knight gave the king a little green book, but he could not read it, because he did not know the letters with which the words were written. He took it, however, and thanked the Green Knight for his kind and hospitable reception. He was very sorry, he assured the knight, that he had disturbed him, as the princess had not meant him at all.

They had to remain overnight in the castle, and the knight

would gladly have kept them longer, but the king insisted that he must leave the next day; so the following morning he said goodbye to his host, and rode back the way he had come until he came to the clearing where the boars were, and from there he went straight home.

The first thing the king did, was to go to the island and take the little green book to his daughter. She was astonished when her father told her about the Green Knight, and gave her his greetings and the book, for she had not thought of a human being, nor had she the faintest idea that a Green Knight existed. But that very evening, when her father was gone, the princess opened her east window and began to read her green book, although it was not written in her mother tongue. The book contained many poems, and its language was beautiful. One of the first things that she read began as follows:

"The wind has risen on the sea,
And bloweth over field and lea,
And while on earth broods silent night,
Who, to the knight, her troth will plight?"

While she was reading the first verse she heard distinctly the rushing of the wind over the water; at the second verse she heard a rustling in the trees; at the third verse her ladies in waiting and all those in or near the palace, fell into a deep slumber. And when the princess read the fourth line, the Green Knight himself flew through the window in the shape of a bird.

Then he resumed his human form, greeted her kindly, and begged her to have no fear. The knight told her that he was the Green Knight whom the king had visited, and from whom he had received the book, and that she herself had brought him thither by reading those lines. She could speak freely to him, and this would relieve her sadness. Then the princess at once felt a great confidence in him, so that she told him her inmost thoughts; and the knight spoke to her with such sympathy and understanding that she felt happy as never before.

Then he said to her that every time she opened the book and read those first verses, the same would come to pass that had happened that evening; everybody on the island would fall asleep except the princess, and he would come to her immediately, although he lived far from her. And the prince also told her that he would always gladly come to her if she really wanted to see him. Now, however, she would better close the book and betake herself to rest.

And at the very moment that she closed the book, the Green Knight disppeared, and the court ladies and all the attendants awoke. Then the princess went to bed and dreamed of the knight and all that he had said to her. When she awoke the next morning she was light-hearted and happy as she had never been before, and day by day her health improved. Her cheeks grew rosy and she laughed and jested, so that all about her were amazed at the change that had taken place in her.

The king said that the evening air and the little green book had really helped her, and the princess agreed with him. But what nobody knew was, that every evening when the princess had read in her book, she received a visit from the Green Knight, and that they had long talks together. On the third visit he gave her a gold ring, and they became betrothed. But not until three months had elapsed could he go to her father and ask her hand in marriage; then he would take her home with him as his beloved wife.

In the meantime the stepmother learned that the princess was growing stronger and more beautiful, and that she was happier than ever before. The queen wondered at this and was vexed, for she had always believed and hoped that the princess would waste away and die, and that then her own daughter would become princess and heiress to the throne.

So one day she sent one of her court ladies over to the island to pay the princess a visit, and to try to find out what was the cause of this remarkable improvement. On the following day the young woman returned and told the queen that it seemed to be particularly helpful to the princess to sit at an open window every evening and read in a book that a strange prince had given her. The evening air had made her drowsy and she had fallen into a deep sleep; the same thing, she said, happened every evening to the court ladies who complained that it made them ill, while the princess became rosier and happier every day. The next day the queen sent her daughter to act as a spy, and told her to pay careful attention to all that the princess did.

"There is some mystery about that window; perhaps a man comes in by it."

The daughter came back the next day, but she could not tell any more than the maid, for she, too, had fallen into a deep sleep when the princess seated herself at the window and began to read.

Then on the third day the stepmother went herself to call on the princess. She was as sweet as honey to her, and pretended to be delighted to see how well she was. The queen questioned her as much as she dared, but could learn nothing from her. Then she went to the east window where the princess was in the habit of sitting and reading every evening, and examined it carefully, but could discover nothing special about it. The window was high above the ground, but vines grew up to it, so that it might have been possible for a very active person to climb up. For that reason the queen took a small pair of scissors, smeared them with poison, and fastened them in the window with their points turned upward, but in such a manner that no one could see them. When evening came and the princess seated herself at the window with the little green book in her hand, the queen said to herself that she would take good care not to fall asleep as the others had done. But her resolve did not help her in the least, for, in spite of herself, when the princess began to read, the queen's eyelids fell and she slept soundly as did the others.

And at that same moment the Green Knight in the form of a bird came in through the window, unseen and unheard by all except the princess. They talked of their love for each other and how there remained only one week of the three months, and then the knight would go to her father's court and ask for her hand in marriage. Then he would take her home, and she would always be with him in his green castle, which lay in the midst of the great woodland realm over which he ruled, and about which he had told her so often.

Then the Green Knight bade his betrothed a tender farewell, resumed the form of a bird, and flew out of the window. But he flew so low that he grazed the scissors that the queen had fastened there, and scratched one leg. He uttered a cry, but disappeared quickly. The princess, who had heard him, sprang up; but in so doing, the book fell from her hand to the floor and closed, and she also uttered a piercing cry which awoke the queen and all the court ladies. They rushed to her and asked what had happened. She answered that nothing was the matter, but that she had only dozed a little, and had been awakened by a bad dream. But that very hour she became ill with a fever and had to go to bed at once. The queen, in the meantime, slipped to the window to get her scissors, and when she found that there was blood on them, she hid them under her apron and took them home.

The princess, however, could not sleep the whole night, and felt miserable all the next day; nevertheless towards evening she rose in order to get a little fresh air. So she seated herself at the open east window, opened the book and read as usual:

"The wind has risen on the sea,
And bloweth over field and lea,
And while on earth broods silent night
Who to the knight her troth will plight?"

And the wind soughed through the trees, and the leaves rustled and all slept, except the princess — but the knight came not. And so the days passed and she waited and watched, and read in her little green book and sang — but no Green Knight came. Then her red cheeks again became pale and her happy heart, sad and heavy; and she began to waste away, to the sorrow of her father, but to the secret joy of her stepmother.

One day the princess walked feebly alone through the castle garden on the island, and seated herself on a bench under a high tree, and there she remained a long time plunged in sad and gloomy thoughts; while she was there two ravens came and perched on a branch over her head, and began to talk together.

"It is pitiful," said one, "to see our dear princess grieving to death for her beloved."

"Yes," said the other one, "especially as she is the only one who can cure him of the wound inflicted on him by the poisoned scissors of the queen."

"How so?" asked the first raven.

"Like cures like," replied the other one. "Over yonder, in the courtyard of the king, west of the stables, there lies, in a hole under a stone, an adder with her nine young. If the princess could get these and cook them, and give three young adders every day to the sick knight, he would recover. Otherwise there is no help for him."

As soon as night came the princess slipped out of the castle, went down to the shore where she found a boat, and rowed over to the palace. She went straight to the stone in the courtyard and rolled it away, heavy as it was, and there she found the nine young adders. These she tied up in her apron, and went forth on the way that she knew her father had taken when he returned from the gathering of the kings.

So she traveled on foot for weeks and months over high mountains and through dense forests, until she came at last upon the same swineherd that her father had met. He pointed out to her the way through the woods to the second herdsman, who in turn showed her the path to the third man. At last she reached the green castle where the knight lived, and lay sick with the poison and a fever, so ill that he recognized nobody, but only rolled and tossed in anguish and pain. Physicians had been called from the ends of the earth, but no one could procure for him the slightest relief.

The princess went into the kitchen and asked whether they could not give her some employment; she would wash the dishes, or do anything they asked her to, if only they would allow her to stay. The cook consented, and because she was so neat and quick and willing at every kind of work, he soon found her a valuable helper, and let her have her own way in many things.

So one day she said to him: "Today you must let me prepare the soup for our sick master. I know very well how it ought to be cooked, but I want to be allowed to cook it alone, and no one may look into the pot."

The cook was willing, and so she cooked three of the young adders in the soup, which was carried up to the Green Knight. And when he had eaten the soup, the fever went down so much that he could recognize those about him and speak intelligently; then he called the cook, and asked him whether he had cooked the soup that had done him so much good. The cook answered that he had done so, as no one else was allowed to prepare the food for his master. Then the Green Knight bade him make more of the same kind of soup on the morrow.

Now it was the cook's turn to go to the princess and beg her to prepare the soup for the knight; and as before, she cooked three young adders in it. This time, after partaking of it, he felt so well that he could get up out of bed. At this, all the doctors were amazed and could not understand how it happened; but, of course, they said that the medicines they had been giving him were beginning to have an effect.

On the third day, the kitchen maid again had to prepare the soup, and she cooked in it the last three young adders. And as soon as the knight had eaten it he felt perfectly well. Then he jumped up and wanted to go down to the kitchen himself to thank the cook, for, after all, he was certainly the best physician.

Now it happened that when he entered the kitchen there was no one there except a maid who was wiping dishes; but even as he looked he recognized her, and it suddenly dawned upon him what she had done for him. He folded her in his arms and said: "It was you then, was it not, who saved my life and cured me of the poison that penetrated into my blood, when I scratched myself on the scissors that the queen had put into the window?" She could not deny it; she was overjoyed, and he also. Soon after that their wedding was celebrated in the green castle; and there they are probably still living together and ruling over all the inhabitants of the green forests.

The King's
Capital

There were once upon a time a man and his wife, and they had one son. They had no money, and sometimes they did not even have bread. When they thought that the boy was old enough to earn his own living, they gave him a crust of bread, and told him to go out into the world to seek his fortune.

The boy went straight to the king's palace and asked whether they would receive him into service. He would do anything they asked him if it were only honest work, and he asked no other wages than his board and lodging. The only place they could find for him was that of errand boy. This suited him very well, for he was quick and nimble on his feet, although not strong enough to do the heavy work of the older serving men. He soon became accustomed to the duties of his new position and gave satisfaction in everything that he undertook. Once he was entrusted with a very important mission. The king was a widower and wanted to marry a rich and beautiful queen with whom he was much in love. As it was very hard to secure admission to her presence, the king commissioned the youth to speak to the queen in his behalf; and so successful was he that he brought back the queen's consent to the marriage, which took place soon afterward. From that time on the errand boy stood high in the king's favor and received fine clothes and good wages.

This excited the anger and jealousy of the court-steward, who was afraid that the errand boy might supplant him; so he sought to devise some plan by which to get the youth out of the way. With that object in view, he one day related to the king that the errand boy had been boasting that he could carry out any command that might be given him, and that even if the king were to send him to hell, in order to collect the interest on his capital, which had long been due but which he had never been able to collect — why he was man enough to do even that!

Now the boy had never said that, nor anything like it, and he told the king so, when he was commanded to appear before him. But all his protestations were of no avail; the king simply told him that he *must* carry out this command, namely, to collect the interest; and as he had a long journey before him he was to be allowed to ride, and received as his steed, a goat.

The errand boy took a bag of provisions, seated himself on the goat, and rode out into the world, letting the animal choose the way. The goat took him into a great forest, and when he had gone some distance, a raven spoke to him and asked him where he was going.

"I must go to hell in order to get the interest for my king," replied the youth.

"That is a long journey and a dangerous one," said the raven, "and if you will follow my advice, dig down to the root of this tree on which I am sitting, and there you will find a sword; and everything that you strike with it will break into pieces. Remember also one thing more, and that is, never leave the highways."

The errand boy dug down to the roots of the tree, and there he found a sword; so he thanked the raven for his good counsel, and went straight along the highway. After a time he met an old woman riding on a goat; this was the devil's grandmother. She rode along beside him, and asked him whether he would not exchange his steed for hers. He said that he would not because he wanted to keep the one that his master had given him. Then she tried to entice him from the straight road on which he was traveling, saying that she knew many good sideroads that would take him much more quickly to his destination. But he steadfastly refused to be persuaded, and at last the old woman left him.

Some time after that he came to a hill on which twelve maidens were standing and weeping. The youth asked them why they were so sad.

"Alas," they said, "we have good reason to weep and lament, for there dwells a terrible monster in our land who is going to devour us at his Christmas banquet."

One of the maidens had a shepherd's pipe in her hand, which the youth took away from her and asked to whom it belonged. They all cried out together that he must not blow it, for otherwise the monster would come at once. Nevertheless the errand boy put the pipe to his lips and blew hard, so that its notes sounded shrilly over hill and dale, and at once the twelve headed monster came roaring toward them. He was indeed horrible to look at, but as soon as the youth touched him with his sword he broke into a thousand pieces which became pebbles. Then the maidens were saved and hastened home, while the young man rode on his way. Again the devil's grandmother came to him and tried to entice him from the straight way, but he remained firm, and she had to go away without having accomplished her purpose.

And again after a time, he came to a hill where he found twenty-four maidens, whom he saved from a monster, as he had saved the first twelve. And again the devil's grandmother tried to tempt him, and again was unsuccessful. And he came to a third hill where were thirty-six maidens, whom he also saved from a monster that was going to devour them. In this manner the young man had saved seventy-two maidens from the three monsters which had seventy-two heads.

Now he went on his way without meeting any more obstacles until he reached the gate of hell. Before it lay a frightful dragon ready to devour anyone who tried to enter. But the raven had prepared the youth for anything that might happen; so following the bird's advice, he spoke to the dragon and bore it greetings from its brother in the woods; and it, knowing that he meant the raven, allowed him to pass unharmed through the gates of hell.

When he entered, the devil started up and asked him gruffly what he wanted. The errand boy greeted him from the king, and said he had come to get the interest that the devil owed him and had not paid for a long time. At first the devil pretended not to know anything about the matter, until his grandmother came and whispered in his ear that he must be careful, for this fellow was dangerous as he had killed his three sons—the many headed monsters. Then he saw that there was nothing for him to do except to comply with the youth's request.

Then the devil immediately became very polite and gave the errand boy all the interest money in a large bag. As he was passing through the gate the dragon called to him and told him to pull off its skin. This he did after some difficulty, and behold there stood before him a most beautiful princess. He put her up behind him, and the goat trotted off tolerably quickly, in spite of his heavy load.

When they had gone a short distance, the princess told him to look back. He did so and saw that the devil and his grandmother, riding on a goat, were pursuing them as fast as they could.

Then the princess turned and spat in the road, and suddenly there was a great lake that the devil could not cross. Then he and his grandmother lay down and quickly drank up all the water.

In the meantime the errand boy and the princess had gained a great deal on them. Again they looked around, and saw the devil coming after them at a great pace. Then the princess threw down a glass bead which immediately became an immense mountain of glass. Now the devil had to return home, in order to rough shoe his goat so that it could cross the mountain.

That, however, took a long time and the fugitives gained a great deal upon their pursuers. When the princess looked around again for the third time, the devil and his grandmother were close on their heels. Then the princess called out: "Let it be bright before us and dark behind!" and at once inky darkness and thick fog fell behind them, whereas bright day lay before them. Now they rode along the highway until they came to the wood, and reached the place where the raven had sat, and given the youth the good advice and the sword. Sure enough, there sat the raven still, and he bade them welcome.

Then the raven said to the young man: "Cut off my head, and put it on again wrong side foremost." And when he had done as he was commanded, there stood, in the place of the raven, a handsome young prince, who was the brother of the princess who had been transformed by magic into a dragon.

Soon afterwards, they all three arrived safe and sound at the king's palace. But as it was night and he did not want to cause any disturbance, the errand boy took the prince and princess upstairs, and showed them two rooms where they could sleep.

That very night it happened that the queen awoke and told the king that she had dreamed that the errand boy had returned, and brought back his two children who had been stolen many years ago.

"Oh, that is only a dream," said the king, "let me sleep."

Soon the queen was awakened again by the same dream, and when the same thing happened for the third time, they both got up, and went down to the stable to look into the goat's stall, and there he was in his old place. Then they went up to the errand boy's room and found him asleep on the floor, and in his bed the young prince, while in the adjoining room the princess lay sleeping.

Then there was boundless joy at the court of the King, who gave his daughter and great riches to the poor errand boy. The court-steward was banished from the country, and the prince reigned over the land with his father until his death, when he ascended the throne himself.

The Princess
in the
Coffin

*T*here were once upon a time a king and a queen who lived in a beautiful palace and ruled over a rich and prosperous country. At first they were very happy, but as the years rolled by and they had no children they became sad.

The king grieved so much about it that at last he said he must go on a long journey to distract his mind. After he had departed, the queen also grieved more and more in her loneliness, until one day her maid came to her, and told her about a wise old woman who had helped many people in their distress. So the queen sent for her, and confided her trouble to her, and immediately the old woman advised her what to do.

"Out in the king's garden, to the left, under the large oak which is nearest to the palace, there is a little greenish brown shrub which bears woolly leaves and has three buds. If the queen will go fasting to this shrub before sunrise and eat the middle bud, she will give birth to a princess in six months. As soon as the child is born she must be entrusted to a nurse whom I will furnish, and live alone with her in an isolated part of the palace. But neither the king nor the queen may see their daughter before her fourteenth birthday, otherwise they will make themselves and their child unhappy."

The queen dismissed the woman after having richly rewarded her, and went down the next morning before sunrise to the little shrub. She plucked and ate the middle bud, and as she bit into it, the bud tasted first sweet, and then bitter as gall. In six months from that time the queen gave birth to a perfectly healthy girl. The nurse, who was in readiness, took the child and went with her into an unoccupied wing of the palace.

When the king returned and learned that the queen had given birth to a child, he was indescribably happy, and wanted to see her at once. But his wife had to hold him back, and tell him that, according to the prophecy, a great misfortune would come upon them all, if the king or the queen should see their daughter before her fourteenth birthday.

That was a long time to wait, for the king longed to see his daughter. And the queen wanted to see her not less than the king; but she knew that the child had not come into the world like other children, and differed from them also in other respects, for she could speak immediately after her birth, and was as wise as a grown person from her infancy. This, and many other things, the queen learned from the nurse with whom she had often spoken about the child; but, in spite of her longing to see her daughter, she heeded the admonitions of the wise woman, and refrained from visiting the little girl. The king, on the other hand, had often lost his patience; and it required all the tact of the queen to divert him from his purpose of going to his daughter's apartments. At length the last day before the fourteenth birthday of the princess arrived.

It happened that on that day the king and the queen were walking together in the garden, when, all of a sudden, the king exclaimed, "I can and will wait no longer; I must see my daughter immediately. A few hours more or less can make no difference." The queen implored him to have patience and wait until the morrow, for as he had waited so long he could certainly wait one day more. But the king would not listen to her and said: "Stop your idle chatter, she is as much my daughter as she is yours, and I *will* see her!" and with these words he rushed straight up to the room of the princess. He tore open the door, pushed aside the nurse who wanted to hold him back, and there he saw the princess, who was the most beautiful young girl imaginable, with clear blue eyes, and the most glorious complexion and golden hair.

The princess fell on her father's neck and kissed him, but at the same time she exclaimed: "Oh, father, father, what have you done! Tomorrow I must die, and you will then be obliged to choose one of three evils: either that your land shall be visited by the black plague, or that it shall be afflicted by a long and bloody war, or that you shall lay me in a plain wooden coffin, which shall be placed in the church and watched by a sentinel, who will mount guard every night for a year."

The king was terrified and believed that the princess was mad. But in order to satisfy her he said, "I will choose the last of the three evils. When you are dead I will lay you away in a plain, wooden coffin, and a sentry shall stand beside it for a year. But *you shall not die*, no matter how ill you may become." And the king sent for all the best physicians in the land, but in spite of all they could do the princess died.

Then the king kept his promise, and gave orders that a sentry should guard his daughter's coffin in the church. When, on the following morning, another soldier came to relieve the man who had been on duty all night, he found no one there, so the people thought that he must have become frightened and run away. But the next evening another sentry was posted, and he, too, disappeared during the night. And thus it continued to happen every night; as soon as they opened the door in the morning they found the church empty, and it was impossible to discover which way the soldiers had gone, if, indeed, they had fled. And what was it that caused them to flee, so that one never saw them, nor heard of them again, from the time that they went on duty?

Now it was universally believed that the princess arose during the night and devoured the sentry; and soon there was no one to be found who was willing to stand guard, for the king's soldiers deserted before their turn came to stand beside the coffin. Then the king promised a large sum of money to the one who would volunteer for sentry duty; and, for a time, the plan was successful, for there were always reckless fellows who wanted the money. But they never received it, for on the morrow they had disappeared like all the rest.

In this manner nearly a year had elapsed, and every night a sentry had stood guard by the coffin, either voluntarily, or by compulsion; but not one of them had ever been seen again. And the same thing had just happened — the sentry had vanished during the night — when a young smith walked into the city in which stood the palace of the King. It was the capital of the country, and all kinds of people came in order to try to get work; and Christian had come for the same reason.

Christian went into an inn to refresh himself with food and drink. In the same room were two sergeants that had been sent out to get somebody to watch beside the coffin of the princess. This they had to do every day, and hitherto they had always been successful; but on that particular day they had found no one. When they saw this strapping young man, they entered into conversation with him, and soon became well acquainted. They ordered food and wine in abundance, and under its influence Christian's tongue soon loosened, and he began to tell what a brave man he was, and that he had never known fear. The sergeants told him that he was just the man for them, and that he could earn a goodly sum of money before he was a day older, for the king would pay a hundred dollars cash to the man who would stand guard at the coffin of his daughter.

That task did not frighten Christian; so, after having drunk another bottle to his courage, he went with the soldiers to the colonel, received a gun and equipment, and was taken to the church and locked in.

He went on duty at eight o'clock, and the first hour or two felt very well pleased at the thought of all the money that he was to have the next day; but, by the time the clock struck eleven the effects of the wine had vanished, and he began to feel decidedly uncomfortable, for he had heard about the sentries who had never returned. These and similar thoughts whirled about through his head, and he made up his mind to try to escape from the church. So he searched everywhere for an exit, and at last found a little wicket gate in the belfry which was unlocked, and through this he planned to flee.

But at the very moment that Christian set his foot upon the threshold of the door, a dwarf stood before him and said, "Good evening, Christian, where are you going so late?" And he felt at once as if he were nailed to the floor, and could move neither hand nor foot.

"Nowhere," answered Christian.

"Oh, yes, you were," said the dwarf, "you were just going to run away without ceremony. But you have given your word to act as sentry tonight, and you *must* remain at your post."

Then Christian replied very humbly that he did not have enough confidence in himself, and begged to be allowed to go.

"Oh, no," said the dwarf, "you *must* remain at your post. But I will give you a piece of good advice: go up into the pulpit and stay there, and do not be frightened at anything that you may see or hear. Nothing can harm you if you stay quietly in the pulpit until you hear the coffin lid close over the corpse. Then all danger will be over, and you can go about in the church wherever you like."

Then the dwarf pushed the young man through the little door and locked it behind him. Christian went up into the pulpit, but nothing happened until the clock struck twelve. Then the lid was thrown from the coffin of the princess, and a terrible ghost, covered with quills like a porcupine, jumped out and screamed, "Guard, where are you, where are you? If you do not come, you shall suffer a more horrible death than anyone before you."

The ghost ran around the church, until at last it saw the man standing in the pulpit. It rushed at him, but could not pass the uppermost steps, and try as it might, it could not reach Christian, who stood trembling in the pulpit. When it struck one, the apparition had to go back to its coffin; and after the coffin lid had fallen into place, a silence of death reigned in the church. Then Christian lay down and fell asleep, and did not awake until aroused by the key being put into the lock. Then he hastened down from the pulpit and took his place, gun in hand, by the coffin of the princess.

It was the colonel himself, who had come with some soldiers, and was not a little suprised to find his new recruit alive and well. He wanted to have a report about what had happened, but Christian would not tell him anything. Then he was brought before the king, who was told that this was the only sentry who had stood guard all night by the coffin of the princess. When the King heard this, he at once gave Christian the hundred dollars and proceeded to question him.

"Did you see anything," he asked, "did you see my daughter?"

"I stood at my post," answered the young smith, "and you must be content with that information, for I did not agree to do anything else." This Christian said, for he did not know whether he dare tell what he had seen and heard, and besides he had become proud because he had done something that nobody had been able to do before him. The king did not insist, but only asked him whether he would act as sentry another night.

"No, I thank you," said Christian, "once is quite enough."

"As you please," said the king, "but you must be hungry after such an experience, so sit down and have some breakfast with me." So a sumptuous repast was brought with many fine wines, to all of which Christian did ample justice; and at last he felt so brave that he told the king that he would guard the coffin the next night if he were paid two hundred dollars.

The king agreed to that, and Christian went out walking with some of the soldiers. His pockets were full of money and he treated them generously, boasting the while about his courage, and saying what pitiful cowards those men were who did not dare to stand guard beside the coffin of the princess. Thus the day passed in eating and drinking until eight o'clock came; then Christian was once more locked up in the church.

But before two hours had elapsed his courage began to ooze away, and he thought that he would try to escape. He found a little door unlocked near the altar, and at ten o'clock he slipped through it and ran as fast as he could to the shore. He had gone about half way, when there stood before him the little man of the previous evening, who said, "Good evening, Christian, where are you going?"

"I have a right to go where I want," answered the smith, but he perceived that he could not stir his feet from the spot.

"No," said the dwarf, "you have agreed to act as sentry, and you *must* remain at your post." Then he took Christian with him, and made him enter the church by the little door through which he had escaped. And when they were inside, the dwarf said to the young man, "Stand before the altar, holding in your hand the prayerbook, and remain standing there until you hear the coffin lid close over the corpse."

Christian at once went to the altar and stood there with the prayerbook in his hand. At twelve o'clock the ghost jumped out of the coffin and screamed, "Sentry where are you, sentry, where are you?" and rushed straight up the pulpit steps. But the sentry was not there that night, so the ghost went screaming and howling about the church until it suddenly saw the smith in his new place. "Ha! are you standing there today?" it screamed, "just wait, and I'll torment you." But it could not reach him, and only screamed and howled until one o'clock, when it went back to the coffin whose lid closed over it.

When everything was quiet in the church, Christian lay down to sleep and did not awake until daylight, when the colonel came to fetch him. He was again led before the king, received his money, but again refused to tell what had happened. At first he declared that he would not serve a third night; but the same persuasive methods being employed as before, Christian at length consented to stand guard, but only on condition that the king should give him the half of his kingdom, for the post was very dangerous indeed. The king agreed to this, and at eight o'clock Christian was locked in the church for the third time. He had not been there an hour when he came to his senses, and thought that he would better leave at once. The king surely did not mean it, when he said that he would give the half of his kingdom to the smith, and besides, in all probability, the third night would be the worst of all. Christian looked around, but found all the gates and doors locked, so he climbed up to one of the windows, and, breaking it, succeeded in crawling through and letting himself down to the ground. Then he ran to the shore, jumped into a boat, and pushed off, laughing the while at the thought of how he had tricked the dwarf this time. But even as he was doing so, he heard the dwarf's voice calling to him from the land, "Good evening, Christian, where are you going?"

Christian did not answer, thinking that he was getting the better of the little man, but rowed vigorously. To his dismay, he noticed that an invisible power had seized the boat and was drawing it to land, in spite of all his frantic efforts with the oars. When he reached the shore, the dwarf seized Christian by the collar and said, "You *must* remain at your post as you promised." And struggle and implore as he might, he had to follow the little man to the church, and climb in through the window that had allowed him to escape. Then the dwarf said to the young man, "Listen carefully to what I shall tell you. Tonight you must lie full length close to the left side of the coffin. The lid is thrown off to the right, and the ghost jumps out on the left. When it has left the coffin and passed over you, you must get into the coffin as quickly as possible, but without letting the ghost see you. And there you must remain until the break of day, no matter whether the apparition addresses you in a rage, or whether it implores you in a mild and affectionate manner. At dawn it will have no power over you, and then you will both be saved."

As soon as Christian was in the church, he lay down beside the coffin and remained there until the clock struck twelve. Then the lid was thrown off to the right, and the ghost of the princess jumped out over him. The smith sprang into the coffin, while the ghost stalked up and down the church, screaming and howling horribly, "Sentry, where are you, sentry, where are you?" Then it rushed to the altar; but finding nobody there, it ran around the church and at last, came back to the coffin. And when it found Christian there, it howled so that the church resounded with its cries, and it screamed, "Now you shall die the most horrible death imaginable." But the young man did not move, so the ghost could not harm him. Nevertheless, it stayed near the coffin, and screamed and sobbed and moaned, so that Christian's hair stood on end, but he did not move. Then it went away for a time, and when it returned he noticed that it now looked like a human being, but white as a sheet. Then it spoke to him, and implored him very sweetly to get up and let it lie down. But the young man said not a word and lay perfectly quiet. Then the ghost vanished just as it struck one.

At the same instant Christian heard beautiful music, which grew louder and louder until its melody filled the whole church. Then he heard the sound of many footsteps, as if the church were filling with people; and then he heard the priests reading the service, and after that the sweetest music that he had ever heard. Then a prayer of thanksgiving was offered to God for delivering the country from pestilence and war, and for rescuing the king's daughter from the power of the evil one; and after that a song of praise was sung, in which the congregation joined. Then he heard his name and that of the princess spoken, as if they were being married. And again he heard the sound of many footsteps, as if the people were leaving the church, while the music, at first full and clear, gradually died away, just as the first rays of the sun shone through the window.

Then the smith leaped from the coffin, and fell on his knees and thanked God. The church was empty, but in front of the altar lay the princess, alive and well, but weeping and trembling with the cold in her shroud. Christian took his soldier's coat and wrapped it about her. Then she wiped away her tears, and gave him her hand, saying that he had saved her from the spell that had been cast over her when her father had violated the command not to visit her before her fourteenth birthday. She also said that if he would marry her she would become his wife; if not, she would go into a cloister. He, however, could not marry another as long as she lived, because they had been married during the service that he had heard in the night. But as you can easily imagine, Christian was only too glad to marry the beautiful young woman who stood before him. Soon the door of the church was opened, and in came, not only the colonel, but also the king himself, for he was very desirous of knowing what had become of the sentry. And there he saw his daughter and the smith sitting together in front of the altar; and he took her in his arms and thanked God and her saviour, and made no objection to her betrothal. Soon after that the wedding was celebrated, and the smith received the half of the kingdom, and ascended the throne soon after the death of the old king.

Many, many years afterward, when the marble floor of the church was being repaired, they found a loose stone under which was a secret vault, and there they found the skeletons of the sentries who had stood guard over the coffin of the princess; and the necks of all were broken. This had been done by the evil spirit that possessed her, and that had drunk three drops of the blood of each victim.

The
Merry Wives

Once there stood three houses in a row, wall to wall. In one lived a tailor, in the next, a carpenter, and in the third, a smith. The three men were married, and their wives were the best of friends. They often told each other what stupid men their husbands were, but they never could agree as to which one of them was the most stupid man; for each one of the women was sure that her husband must be the most stupid.

The three women used to go to church together every Sunday, and on the way they had a good opportunity to chat and gossip together. After the service they always stopped at a little tavern where they had a measure of brandy together. Now at that time a measure cost three shillings, so each woman had to pay one shilling. After a time the price of spirits went up so that a measure cost four shillings. That they did not like at all, as there were only three of them, and no one of them wanted to pay the extra shilling.

So one day on the way home from church they talked the matter over and agreed that the woman whose husband was the most stupid and allowed the worst trick to be played on him, need not pay for her drink thereafter.

The next day the tailor's wife said to her husband, "I have engaged some girls to come here tomorrow to card wool, for there is much to be done and we have to hurry. Now in the evening the young men will be sure to come, and the young people will want to have their fun together, so, of course, no work will be done then. If only we had a rather vicious dog we could easily keep the fellows away."

"Yes," said her husband, "that is very true."

"Listen," she continued, "you could act as watch-dog and frighten the young men away from the house."

The man hardly thought that he could; nevertheless, he yielded to his wife's entreaties. So towards evening, she fastened some woolly skins about him, drew a wool cap over his head, and fastened him with a chain to their kennel. There he stood and growled and barked at everybody that approached, and his neighbors' wives amused themselves famously with him.

On the following day when the carpenter came home from his work, his wife clasped her hands and exclaimed, "For heaven's sake, husband dear, what is the matter with you? you are certainly sick." But he had not the faintest idea that anything was the matter with him; all that he knew was that he was very hungry. So he seated himself at the table and began to eat; but his wife who sat opposite him, shook her head and looked very sad.

"Dear, you are looking worse and worse; you are very pale, and I can see clearly that something serious is the matter with you." Now the man began to become uneasy himself, and to think that he was not well. "It is really high time that you should go to bed," said his wife; at last she succeeded in getting him to go to bed. She covered him up well and gave him hot drinks, and finally the man said that he really felt wretched. "You will certainly never recover from this illness, my poor husband," said the woman, "I am sure that you are going to die." Soon after that she said, "Now we shall have to bid each other farewell, for death has set his seal upon you, and now I must close your eyes for you are dead." And as she spoke, she did so. The foolish carpenter, who believed all that his wife said, believed that he was dead and lay perfectly quiet, letting his wife do what she wished.

She then called in her neighbors, and they helped her put her husband in a coffin — it was one that he had made himself. This the woman had prepared very comfortably; she had bored holes in the lid, so that her husband might have air, made a soft bed for him to lie on, and then covered him up with a warm blanket. She folded his hands on his breast, but instead of putting a bible or a hymn-book in them, she gave him a bottle of brandy. After the man had lain there a short time, he took a swallow of the liquor, then another and yet another, until he fell into a deep sleep and dreamed that he was in heaven.

In the meantime all the people of the village had learned that the carpenter had died and was to be buried on the following day. Meanwhile what did the smith's wife do? Her husband had come home intoxicated, and had fallen asleep. While he was sleeping, his wife daubed him with pitch from top to toe, and let him sleep until late the next forenoon, when the pallbearers and the funeral procession were already on the way to the church with the coffin. Then the smith's wife rushed in to her husband and woke him, saying that he had overslept himself and must hurry if he wanted to reach the church in time to pay his last respects to his friend. The smith was confused for he knew nothing about a funeral, but his wife hurried him, explaining to him the while that the carpenter had died the day before.

"But," said the smith, "I must put on my black suit."

"You fool," said the wife, "you have it on already, do hurry up and go."

So the smith ran and as he approached the procession, he called to the people to wait for him. They looked around and seeing the black figure running toward them, thought it was the devil. That frightened them nearly to death, so that they threw down the coffin and ran away as fast as they could. As it crashed to the ground the lid flew off, and the carpenter awoke and sat up to look out and see what was going on. Then he remembered what had taken place, and knew that he was dead and had to be buried. He recognized the smith, and said in a feeble voice, "Dear neighbor, if I were not already dead I should certainly laugh myself to death, to see you come to my corpse in that guise."

From that time on, the carpenter's wife never had to pay for her measure of brandy, for they all had to acknowledge that she had made the worst fool of her husband.

The Treasure

There was once a poor peasant who tilled a small field that belonged to a rich landowner. One day while he was ploughing, his plough struck something so violently that it could not be moved. At first the man thought that it was a stone, but when he looked more carefully he found that it was a large chest full of old coins. It was gold and silver money that had probably been hidden there many hundred years ago in war times.

The peasant filled a bag with the money and dragged it home, for he thought that he had as good a right to keep the money as anyone else. The original owner had, of course, died many generations ago. In spite of that, he feared that the landowner would claim and seize the money when he learned that it had been found in his field. So the peasant said nothing to anybody except his wife about the find, and he begged her to keep silent about it.

But she could not keep the secret, and had to tell some of her friends about the good fortune. To be sure she asked each one separately not to tell anybody; but as they could not keep the secret either, at last the news of the discovery of the treasure came to the ears of the landowner.

Soon after that he rode out to the peasant's cottage, which lay far out on a lonely heath. There was, however, nobody at home except the woman, for her husband had just gone to town to get some money changed. So when the landowner asked the woman about the matter, she told him all that she knew — that her husband had found a chest full of money out in the field, and that he was not at home now, and that she did not know where he had put the money. The owner then said that he would return another time, and make further inquiry about the money.

When the peasant came home, his wife told him all that had happened; nevertheless, he did not reproach her. The next day he took his horses and wagon and asked his wife to accompany him to the town. There he exchanged all his old money for new coins, and invested the proceeds carefully and to good advantage. Then be bought a bushel of little rolls, which he put into a large bag. The man and his wife ate and drank to their hearts content, and towards evening they started on their homeward journey.

It was late in the autumn, and it was raining and blowing hard as they drove home in the dark. But the wine she had drunk had gone to the head of the wife, and she slept soundly on the back seat. After they had gone for some distance, she was awakened by a roll that fell on her head, and immediately after that another one fell into her lap; and as soon as she fell asleep, rolls again began to rain down upon her. These her husband was throwing into the air so that they should fall upon her.

"But what is happening?" the woman called to her husband, "it seems to me that it is raining rolls."

"Yes," said her husband, "that is just what it is doing; we are having terrible weather."

As they were passing the landowner's house, the woman was awakened by the braying of an ass.

"What was that?" she exclaimed, feeling very uneasy.

"Well, I hardly like to say," replied her husband, "but if I must tell the truth, it was the devil who once loaned our landlord some money, and is now tormenting him because he will not pay the interest; he is thrashing him with a horsewhip."

"Hurry up," said the woman, "and get away from here as fast as you can." So the man whipped up his horses, and at last they reached home safe and sound.

But when they were home the husband said, "Listen, wife, I

heard some bad news when we were in town. The enemy is in our land and this night he will be in our neighborhood. So you must crawl into the potato-cellar in order to be out of danger, while I shall stay up stairs and protect our property as well as I can."

So the peasant's wife went down into the cellar, while her husband took his gun and went outside, and shot and cried out and made a great noise. This he kept up all night, and towards morning he told his wife that she could come up. "Fortunately," he said, "I was able to hold my own. I shot down many of the enemy, who at last were compelled to retire, taking with them their dead and wounded."

"Thank God," she said, "that everything has turned out well; I was frightened nearly to death."

A few days after that the landowner rode out and found the peasant standing before his cottage. "Where is the treasure that you found in my field?" he asked him. The man answered that he did not know anything about a treasure.

"Oh, nonsense," said the landowner, "it will not do you any good to deny it, for your wife told me all about it herself."

"That is quite possible," said the man, "for my wife is sometimes a little queer, and one can not always believe all that she says." And he touched his forehead as he spoke.

Then the landowner called the woman and asked whether it were not true that she had confessed to him that her husband had found a chest full of money in the field.

"Certainly," she said, "and I was with him in town when he exchanged the old money for new coins."

"When was that?" asked the landlord.

"Why that was the time we had the frightful storm when it rained bread rolls."

"Nonsense," said he; "when was that?"

"It was on the day of the great battle that was fought on our field, after the enemy had invaded our country."

"What battle, and what enemy?" said the landlord, "I think that the woman is crazy. But tell me at once, when was it that you were in town to exchange the money?"

Then the woman wept, and much as she disliked to do so, she had to say it: "It was the same evening that the devil was tormenting you and beating you because you would not pay him what you owed him."

"What are you saying?" screamed the landowner, in a rage; "I'll thrash you for your lying nonsense." And with that he gave her a blow with his whip and dashed out of the door and rode away, and never again asked about the treasure. The peasant, however, bought a large farm in another part of the country and lived there happily with his wife.

The
Old Man
Who Had a
Large Family

There was once a very old man who had four hundred and twenty-seven sons. When they were grown they went to their father and said that they wanted to get married, and asked him how they should go about it. "Let me attend to the matter," he said, "I understand such things better than you do, and will find a wife for each one. Saddle my old horse, and I will ride forth to woo for you."

But the old man had to ride far before he discovered a man who had four hundred and twenty-seven daughters, all unmarried. At last, however, he found such a man, and stopped at his house and told him that he had come to ask the young women to marry his sons.

At last they came to an understanding, and agreed that the young people should live with the father of the sons, while the other man was to bear the expenses of the wedding and of the young women's outfit. When the business was concluded the old man asked the servant to saddle and lead out his horse.

"Has he been fed?" he asked; "I have a long journey before me, and do not want to stop on the way to feed him."

"Yes," replied the servant, "I think that he has had enough to eat, for I have given him seven bales of hay."

"Has he had anything to drink?"

"No, I did not have time to give him anything."

"Never mind, I shall pass some pond or lake and it will not take long to water him."

The old man rode away and soon came to a lake. The horse walked into it and began to drink, and before long he had drained it because he was very thirsty. On the bottom there were many fishes left, and a multitude of birds flew down and carried them away. And as the old man sat on his horse and looked up to see where the birds were carrying their booty, something fell into his eye. He tried to get it out, but was not successful. So there was nothing for him to do but to ride home as fast as he could, holding his hand before his eye, which pained him very much.

As soon as the father got home he told his sons that he had been lucky enough to get a bride for each one of them, but that he had been so unfortunate as to have something fall into his eye, which they would have to help him remove. They searched and searched, but could find nothing. At last the eldest son, who was very clever, said, "We will put our boats into your eye and sail around until we find the thing." That they did, and for seven days they sailed about until at last they found the thing that they were looking for. And it turned out to be a large fish bone that a bird had dropped. So they pulled it out, and took away their boats, and the old man was comfortable once more.

Then the men had to find a carpenter who would make them four hundred and twenty-seven bedsteads for the four hundred and twenty-seven couples. And the fish bone was so large that the carpenter was able to make posts for the four hundred and twenty-seven beds.

When they were all ready, the old man one day thought that he would like to lie down and take a nap on one of the beds; so he put on his red night cap, and stretched himself out. When he was nearly asleep, a fox sneaked in, and began to gnaw at one of the bedposts. And it seemed to him that it tasted of birds and fish. That, however, made the old man angry, and he took off his red cap and threw it at the fox, which was so frightened that it jumped up and hid itself in the man's beard.

The old man tried to seize the fox as it slipped into his beard, but could not catch it; and later on it was quite impossible to find the animal. Then he called his sons to help him find the fox. The oldest son now suggested that each son take his scythe and cut off some of the beard. So for seven days the four hundred and twenty-seven sons mowed until they found the fox in its hiding place, where it had installed itself very comfortably and had given birth to seven young ones.

At last everything was arranged in a satisfactory manner, and the four hundred and twenty-seven sons and their father, went to the home of the father of the four hundred and twenty-seven young women, and a great wedding was celebrated which lasted four hundred and twenty-seven days.

Hans
and
Gretchen

Some distance from a little village stood a small cottage, in which lived a man and his wife and their only daughter, whose name was Gretchen. The people were poor and honest and Gretchen was good and industrious, and very pretty.

Near the village was many a large and fertile farm; but the finest and richest was the one that Hans was to inherit. His father had died long ago, and the farm was managed by his mother, who was faithfully assisted by her son. He had to wait until he was twenty years old, and then the whole estate would be turned over to him. Hans was not only the richest, but also the best and the handsomest young man in the village, so that it was no wonder that the maidens thought much of him, and Gretchen also, like all the rest.

Early one morning Hans came to the kitchen when Gretchen happened to be alone, and said to her: "Listen, Gretchen; you are a pretty good girl, and I should like to marry you sometime, if you can remain silent and not say a word to anybody about it."

"I thank you," said Gretchen, "but you should not say such a thing to anyone."

Hans went away and Gretchen remembered that she had to bake some bread for breakfast. So she took some flour and ashes and began to mix them. Just then her mother entered and seeing what her daughter was doing, exclaimed in astonishment, "Why Gretchen, what are you doing?"

"Oh, mother!" she cried, "I am so happy."

"What are you so happy about?" asked the mother.

"Hans has just been here," said Gretchen, "and asked me to be his wife, if I could be silent and not tell anybody about it."

"He ought really not to speak that way to anyone," said the mother, and threw away the dough.

Now the father came out to see why he had to wait so long for his breakfast, and the women told him the reason for their happiness. Then he went out, and harnessed the horses to the wrong end of the wagon, and drove away. Soon he met Hans, who asked him what was the matter.

"Oh, I am so happy!" said the man.

"Why are you so happy?" asked Hans.

"Because you said that you wanted to marry my daughter," replied the man.

"Yes I said that—if she could keep quiet about it; but she evidently cannot." And Hans went angrily on his way.

Many days passed without their seeing Hans. At last they learned that he had been wooing the daughter of a rich peasant, and that the banns were to be published on the following Sunday. They were published the first time and the second time; but before they were to be published for the third and last time, Gretchen said to her mother, "I must go to church today in order to see my beloved once more at communion."

And when they had received the communion and were going back to their places, Gretchen whispered to Hans as she passed him, "I have not yet lost faith in you."

His betrothed who was, of course, in church that morning, asked Hans who the girl was that whispered to him as she went by. "Oh that was a girl that I once thought of marrying, if she had been able to keep a secret."

"Such a thing never happened to me," said his betrothed, "could she not remain silent? Why I have had seven different suitors and have never said a word about it to anybody—oh goodness! except this time, when it slipped out unawares." When Hans heard this he jumped up and ran away, and she never saw him again. He married Gretchen after all, and they lived happily together for many years.

Miracle

There was once a king who married when very young and whose life was extremely happy. But his happiness only lasted a short time, for after he had been married about a year he lost his beloved wife, who died soon after giving birth to a little girl. When she knew that death was near, she asked the king to promise her to remain a widower for seven years, and if at the end of that time he wanted to marry again, he should choose no other woman as his wife than the one his daughter should wish to have for her mother.

This the king promised to his wife and soon after that she died, to his great grief, for they had always been devoted to each other, and had lived very happily together. A nurse was found for the little princess, who grew in mind and body; and the nurse was so good and kind, and so full of motherly care and tenderness for the royal child that it seemed that it would have been impossible for a mother to have been more loving.

And the princess grew to love her nurse as if she were her own mother. But all this apparent love on the part of the nurse was nothing but clever calculation and dissimulation; for as the child grew older, the woman would often say how sad it would be for them both when they had to separate, and how beautiful it would be if they could always live together. And when the princess had attained her seventh year, the nurse spoke out without any attempt at concealment and said that probably her father, the king, would soon ask her to advise him whom to marry, and to tell him whom she would prefer to have as her mother; and to this she must answer that she loved her nurse best, because otherwise she might have a step-mother who would be unkind to her.

And everything came to pass as the crafty nurse had expected. Soon after the princess was seven years old, she asked her father to marry the nurse. This he did, as he believed that he had to fulfill the promise that he had made to his wife. And so the nurse became queen; but from that moment all the love that she had pretended to feel for the princess, vanished utterly. The queen herself had a daughter, whom she now brought to court, and who tried to supplant the king's daughter wherever possible. Besides that, the wicked stepmother did everything that she could to make the king hate his own child. Every day she would accuse the poor girl of some bad thing that she had never done. The king heard nothing but good of his stepdaughter, and nothing but evil of his own daughter. He often scolded her, but did not lose his affection for her; nevertheless, the princess grew timid and began to fear her father, and appeared before him as little as possible.

Matters stood thus when the princess was fifteen years old; and to make things worse for her, it happened that the king had to go away for a time to wage war against another country. During his absence the queen was to rule and to conduct the affairs of state. But the wicked woman spent much time trying to devise ways and means to separate the father and daughter permanently, so that the princess would be put entirely out of the way, and the queen's daughter be able to take her place. Now, in spite of her ingenuity, the wicked queen could not think of any plan by which to accomplish her purpose, and she was in a very bad humor because she had learned that the king was soon to return. One day while she was walking in the woods, deep in her evil thoughts, she met an old witch, who asked her why she was so depressed, and wanted to know whether she could not help her. The queen told her trouble to the witch, who promised to find a way out of it if she would meet her at the same spot the next day.

The queen went to the place appointed and found the witch

awaiting her. The old woman had, in the meantime, milked all the wild animals of the forest, and had made of this milk a small cheese, which she gave to the queen. This cheese she was to give to her step-daughter to eat. But the princess must eat it of her own free will, else it would avail nothing. The queen took the cheese home and laid it in a place where the princess would be sure to see it. And as soon as the princess had seen the cheese she exlaimed, "What a nice little cheese, I must taste it." And it tasted so good that she ate it all. But soon she began to feel ill, and day by day she lost her beauty.

When the king came home the queen went to meet him, and he immediately asked her about his daughter. Then the hypocritical woman looked sad and begged the king not to be too angry with his daughter, or to deal too harshly with her, but, really, it could not be denied that she had behaved very badly during his absence. Then the king sent for the princess.

He did not speak a word to her but ordered two of his faithful servants to put her in a carriage, and take her far into the woods where no human beings ever came. Then they were to kill her, and as proof that they had fulfilled his command, they were to bring to him her heart, her little finger, and her blood-soaked garments.

The poor princess did not know what her father's refusal to speak to her meant, for she was conscious of nothing but that she felt very sick and miserable. Then the servants took her deep into the woods, where they told her that she must die as her father, the king, had commanded. But the princess begged the servants to spare her life, and promised them that she would never go back to her father's kingdom. Then they had compassion on her and said that they would spare her life; so they killed a young deer that had broken its leg, and cut out its heart; they also soaked some of the garments of the princess in its blood, and then she had to sacrifice one of her little fingers.

The servants now went back to the palace with the bloody

proofs, while the princess went deeper and deeper into the forest. It was an immense forest which separated the king's realm from another country, and she continued to walk until she came out on the other side. But all the animals of the forest flocked about her, deer, hares, foxes, but especially the wild beasts. To all these it seemed as if the girl were one of themselves. They did her no harm but swarmed around her so that she could hardly go forward, and all the time she was in terror lest they should tear her to pieces. The princess hurried on as fast as she could, but towards evening she was exhausted and sank down under a tree; after a short rest she summoned her remaining strength and climbed up into the tree, in order to be able to spend the night safe from the unwelcome attentions of the animals.

Once in the tree the princess found a large hollow place, where she was able to recline and be comfortable, and soon she fell asleep and slept sweetly until daybreak. When she a-woke she was trembling with cold, but felt wonderfully strengthened and refreshed by her sleep, and when she looked at herself she found that she looked as she did before her illness. The joy of the princess was very great, and she hastened down from the tree and went to the edge of the forest where she could look out into the open country.

But as her eyes wandered over the strange landscape, her loneliness and sad condition were borne in upon her more than ever, and she burst into tears and prayed God to help her in her distress.

Just then the young woman heard a voice behind her which said, "Here I am, mother, wait and take me with you." She looked all about her, but could see nothing but a little black dog that came running toward her, barking and wagging his tail. And he it was that had called her mother. "You must call me Miracle," he said, "and you need not weep or have any more care, for I shall see that you lack nothing."

Miracle went in advance and led the princess back for a short distance into the forest until they reached a hill covered with beautiful shade trees, and from which a little brook bubbled forth.

"Little mother," asked Miracle, "would you not like to live here?"

"Yes indeed," she replied, "but what am I to live in?"

"You will see in a few minutes," and thereupon Miracle dug with his paws and bit branches from the trees with his sharp teeth, and soon he had built a neat little cottage. Then he collected a pile of dry grass and leaves and said: "Lie down a little while and rest, mother; I shall soon be back again."

The land that the princess could see from her hill was ruled by a prince who was the neighbor of her father; the forest through which she had passed was the boundary between their dominions, and not far from her cottage was the royal palace where the prince lived.

The little black dog ran to the palace and all the gates and doors opened, as soon as he scratched them with his little paws. And he went to the housekeeper of the palace and said, "My name is Miracle, and I want you to give me some bed clothes and pillows for my mother; she is out in the woods and is cold." Then the housekeeper threw him some old rags, but he would not touch them. "Keep your rags," he said, and running to the bedroom of the prince he took the bedclothes that were on his bed, and ran back to the princess.

"There, mother," he said, "now make your bed, while I go out and get you something to eat." Then the little black dog ran back to the palace and went into the kitchen.

"My name is Miracle," he said, "and I want some food for my mother who is starving in the woods." Then the cook threw him some bones.

"Keep those bones," said the dog, "I would not condescend to accept anything from you." Jumping up on to the kitchen table, he seized the silver platter containing a roast intended for the prince, and carried both off to the princess in the woods.

"I'll come right back," he said, and again ran to the palace. This time Miracle ran to the wine cellar of the palace, and brought back the drinking horn of the prince filled with the finest wine. For a long time the princess lived in her little cottage on the hill, while Miracle brought her all that she needed from the palace of the prince.

Until now we have only spoken of two kingdoms; but there was still another one, situated beyond the prince's country. Over this land ruled an old king who had three daughters, each one of whom seemed to be uglier and more malicious than the others. They would have liked to marry, but their father insisted that they should accept no one of a rank lower than prince. But no suitors presented themselves, and so the years went by and the princesses became older and uglier and more malicious.

Now it happened that the prince from whose palace Miracle brought all the good things, was a young, unmarried man, whose realm was much smaller than that of his neighbor, the old king. One day the king sent an embassy to the prince to inquire whether he would not like to marry one of his daughters; he could choose the one that he preferred. The prince sent back a reply that he did not want to marry any one of them. That was a great insult to the old king, who swore that he would be avenged; so he declared war against the prince, whose land he invaded with his army. A battle was fought in which the king was victorious and the prince taken prisoner. He was thrown into a dungeon where he was kept for several days. Then came a messenger from the king and said: "My lord the king has commanded me to inform you that you deserve to suffer death for the insult that you have offered him; nevertheless, he is willing to show you mercy and grant you your life and land on condition that you marry one of his daughters." But the prince answered him curtly that he would never do this; and that, as he had not done it voluntarily, he would certainly not do it under compulsion. So sentence of death was passed and the day of his execution fixed.

While the prince was sitting sad and lonely in his dungeon, a little dog came suddenly to him, and it was none other than our acquaintance, Miracle. He spoke to the prince and asked him whether he would not like to leave his prison.

"Of course I would," answered the young man.

"Well," said Miracle, "if you will marry my mother, I can and will set you free."

"Your mother," said the prince, "who and what is she, and what does she look like?"

"My name is Miracle, and that is her name also, for we are of the same blood."

"No, I thank you," said the prince, "marry a dog! I will not do that any more than I would marry one of those malicious, old princesses."

Immediately Miracle vanished. But the day before the execution he again appeared before the prince and said, "Well, have you reflected and made up your mind whether you will marry my mother, and gain your life, freedom and realm? Otherwise, as you well know, all will be over tomorrow."

"If she were only a woman, and not one of those wretched old princesses, I would marry her and thus win my freedom and land; but a dog — that is not to be thought of."

"As you are willing to marry my mother," said Miracle, "you must have her bridal robes made at once and have her measure taken by a dressmaker." When the prince heard that, he no longer refused, for he knew that his bride must be a human being. Nevertheless, it seemed strange to him that the dog should speak of having wedding robes made, when it was evident from the position of the prince that he could not attend to such matters.

The next day the execution was to take place. Soldiers were

sent to the tower to fetch the prince and lead him to the place of execution, where the gallows had been erected and the hangman was waiting. As the prisoner was led up to the gallows, Miracle ran between the legs of the guards and called out, "Either set the prince free at once and take him home to his realm, or I will tear you all to pieces, for he is to marry mother."

But they called him an impudent puppy and laughed him to scorn, and the executioner gave him a kick. Then, however, Miracle became angry and showed them what he could do. He rushed at the bystanders and tore them to pieces, and soon not only the hangman and soldiers, but also the king and all his court lay dead around the gallows. Then Miracle went back with the prince to his realm, and did not stop until they reached the little cottage on the hill where the princess lived.

A strange feeling came over the prince as he followed the dog, but as soon as he entered the cabin and saw the beautiful princess, a great weight seemed to fall from his heart. With joy he greeted her as his betrothed and declared that their wedding should be celebrated in three days.

Then Miracle said to the prince, "You are at liberty to invite anybody you please to the wedding, but I reserve the right to invite one single guest." Permission was granted him, and the guest he asked was none other than the father of the princess. Then Miracle continued and said, "After the marriage ceremony you will sit down to the wedding feast, and I will come sit under the table next to the guest whom I have invited. Every time that he wants to partake of the food that is placed before him, I shall jump up and take it away from him. For a time he will not say anything but take something else; at last, however, he will become angry and ask whether you are trying to make a fool of him. Then you must say that you are sorry that he has been offended by anyone in your palace, even if it were but your dog, and that you are willing that he should draw his sword and kill the animal if it should annoy him again. Now promise me that you will comply with my request." The prince promised, and sent out messengers to invite the guests, and made preparations for the wedding.

The day came, and the marriage was celebrated with great pomp and splendor. The bride with her golden crown on her head, was radiant with happiness and indeed fair to gaze upon; but, of course, her father did not recognize her, for he thought her dead, and, besides, he had not seen her since her fifteenth year. And the little black dog came and seated himself at the feet of the old king, and every time that he wanted to partake of any food the dog snapped it away from him.

For a time the king said nothing, but at last he lost his patience, and said that he had not come to this wedding to be made a fool of. The dog had surely been brought in to annoy him, for it was certainly not the custom to allow dogs in a royal banquet hall. Then the bridegroom answered that he regretted deeply that the dog had acted thus towards the royal guest, and that much as he loved the animal he was quite willing that the king should punish him as he saw fit. The king in a rage drew his sword, and split the dog's skull, and suddenly in his place stood a handsome little boy, who said, "Here I am grandfather! take me in your arms and carry me to my mother who is sitting at the end of the table."

The old king arose as if in a dream, but nevertheless he did as the boy had bidden him and carried him to the bride, in whom he recognized his daughter whom he had once commanded to be killed. Then the child told the whole story of the wickedness of the old king's wife, and of what had happened to the princess, and all were glad that her troubles were at an end. Then the king gave orders to a messenger to go back to his kingdom, and say that the wicked queen and her daughter should be driven from the palace into the great forest. This was done and they were never heard of again, for the wild beasts tore them to pieces and devoured them.

The
Wizard's
Daughter

There was once a boy who went out to find work; and as he was going along he met a man who asked him where he was going.

"I want to find something to do to earn my living," he answered.

"Then come with me," said the man, "I need just such a boy as you are, and will pay you good wages. You shall receive a bushel of money the first year, two bushels the second, and three bushels at the end of the third year, for you must serve me for three years and obey me in everything, no matter how strange it may seem to you. But you need never have any fear of the things that I command you to do, for there is no danger connected with them if you follow my directions exactly."

The boy consented, and followed the man to his house. It was a strange dwelling, for he lived on a hill in the midst of a dense forest; and the boy saw no other human being than his master, who was a mighty wizard and had great power over men and beasts, so that he was feared by all.

On the following day the boy had to begin his service. His first task was to feed all the wild animals that the wizard had charmed. There were bears, and wolves, and stags, and hares, that the wizard had gathered into herds, and kept captive in his great stables that extended under the earth for over a mile. The boy finished his work in one day, and the wizard praised him and told him that he was doing his work very well.

The next morning the wizard said to him, "Today the animals do not need to be fed, as they do not receive food every day, so I will let you play until they have to be fed again." Thereupon

the wizard uttered a few words that the boy did not understand, and in the twinkling of an eye, he was changed into a
hare, and ran off into the woods.

He was now very quick and nimble, and, indeed that was
very necessary, for he had to run a great deal; whoever happened to see him wanted to shoot him, and the dogs pursued him
barking, whenever they came upon his tracks. As the wizard
had all the other animals in his stables under ground, the hare
was the only animal in the forest, so the hunters were very desirous of catching or killing him. But they were not successful,
for there was no dog that could catch him, nor any hunter that
could hit him. This was, however, a very unrestful kind of life;
but at last he became used to it when he perceived that there
was no danger in it for him, and, indeed, he rather enjoyed
making game of the hunters.

A year passed thus, and when it had elapsed the wizard called
him home, for he was now in his power like all the other animals. The wizard again uttered a few words, and the hare became a man once more. "Well," said the wizard, "how are you
satisfied with your position, and how do you like to be a hare?"

"Oh, I like it very well," said the boy, "I never could run so
quickly before."

Thereupon the wizard showed him the bushel of money he
had earned, and the boy was pleased and concluded that he
would stay another year in the service of the wizard.

On the first day of his second year he had to do the same work
as the previous year; that is he had to feed all the animals in the
wizard's stable. And when he had done that, the wizard again
uttered a few words over him, and the boy was changed into a
raven and flew high into the air. That pleased him immensely,
for now he could go much faster and further than when he was
a hare, and fly around for his pleasure, as there were no dogs to
hunt and worry him. But soon he perceived that even in the air
he was not free from danger, for whenever the hunters spied

him they would shoot at him, as he was the only bird that was to be seen far and wide, the wizard having caught all the others.

But he soon became accustomed to it for nobody could hit him; and so he flew and enjoyed himself until the second year was up, when the wizard called him home and gave him back his human form.

"Well, how do you like to fly about as a raven?" asked the wizard.

"Very well," the boy answered, "because I never was able to fly so high before."

Then the wizard showed him the two bushels of money that he had earned, and they stood beside the bushel he had earned the first year. And the boy gladly remained a third year in the service of the wizard.

On the following day the boy performed his accustomed task, that of feeding the wild animals. And when it was done the wizard transformed him into a fish swimming in a brook in the woods. He swam up and down the stream, drifted with the current, and at last swam out to sea. And he swam further and further until he came to a glass castle, which was built at the bottom of the ocean. The fish could look into all the splendidly furnished rooms and halls; all the furniture was made of white whalebone inlaid with gold and pearls, and on the floor were soft carpets that resembled the finest moss; and there were also flowers and trees with strangely curved twigs and branches, which were of various colors—green, yellow, red and white. And little fountains bubbled up out of pretty shells, and their water fell into other shells that were as clear as crystal, and made music that filled the whole castle. But the most beautiful of all was a young girl who wandered about the castle alone. The young girl went from one room to another, and one could see that she did not take any pleasure in all the splendor that surrounded her. She went about sadly, and it never seemed to enter her mind to look at her reflection in the polished walls of glass, although she was the most beautiful creature that one could conceive. And the boy thought so too, as he swam round and round the castle and looked in from all sides.

"How I wish I were a man now instead of being a poor, stupid fish," said the boy to himself. "If I could only think of the words that the wizard utters when he transorms me." And he swam, and thought, and reflected, until at last the magic formula came to him. At once he tried it, and that selfsame moment he stood— a man—at the bottom of the sea.

Then the young man hastened into the glass castle and spoke to the young girl, who at the sound of his voice was at first almost frightened to death. Then he explained to her how he had come down there, and spoke to her so kindly that she soon recovered from her fright, and was very glad indeed to have him as a companion, for the solitude was awful. But the time passed so quickly for both, that the young man—for he was now a man grown—had quite forgotten how long he had been in the castle.

One morning the maiden said to him that it was about time for him to be changed back into a fish, for the wizard would soon call him home and he would then have to go. But before the young man resumed the form of a fish the young woman told him that she was the daughter of his master, the wizard, and that he had imprisoned her in the castle at the bottom of the sea in order that he might be sure that she was perfectly safe. In the meantime the wizard's daughter had devised a plan whereby she and the young man might be able to see each other again, and perhaps even secure permission to get married. But in order to succeed it would be necessary for the youth to be very careful and do exactly as she should tell him.

The maiden told him that the kings of all the lands round about the wizard, owed him money, and that it was the turn of the king of the kingdom whose name she now mentioned to him, to pay his debt; and if he could not pay at the proper time he would be beheaded. "And he cannot pay," she said, "That I know. First of all you must leave the service of my father, for the three years are up, and you are at liberty to go. So take your six bushels of money and go to the kingdom about which I have just told you, and enter the service of the king. When the time for the payment of the debt draws nigh, you will easily notice it for the king will be in a very bad humor. Then you must tell him that you know very well what is worrying him; that it is the money that he owes the wizard, but cannot pay. But you can loan it to him, for it amounts to exactly six bushels. You must, however, loan him the money on one condition only, and that is that he shall take you along as his court jester when he calls on my father. When you reach the palace of the wizard, you must play all kinds of tricks, breaking windows, and doing all the mischief possible. That will make my father furious; and as the king is responsible for all the actions of his jester, the wizard will sentence him to death in spite of the fact that he has paid his debt, unless he can answer correctly questions that my father will put to him. The first question that my father will ask, will be: 'Where is my daughter?' Then you must step forth and say, 'She is at the bottom of the sea.' He will also ask whether you can recognize her, and you must answer, 'Yes.' Then a large number of young women will be led past you in order that you may point out which one you take to be his daughter. As you might not recognize me, I shall nudge you as I pass, and you must immediately seize me and hold me fast. The wizard's next question will be, 'Where is my heart?' and you must again step forward and answer, 'It is in a fish.' He will then ask, 'Do you know this fish?' and you must answer, 'Yes.' Then he will have all kinds of fish appear before you, and you will have to choose the right one from among them. But I will take good care to be by your side and when the right fish comes I will touch you gently, and you must seize him and quickly cut him open. Then the wizard will be discouraged and will ask you no more questions."

The young man remembered carefully all that his beloved had told him, and then tried to think what the magic formula was that the wizard used to transform him. At first he could not remember it and was much frightened, but after a time it came to him and he changed himself quickly into a fish, and swam back through the sea to the brook in the forest. Soon he was called by the wizard who changed him back again into a human being.

"Well," he asked the young man, "how did you enjoy swimming around as a fish?"

"I liked it better than anything else," answered the youth, and that was certainly quite true, as we all know. Thereupon the wizard showed him the three bushels of money which he had earned during the last year, and which stood beside the other three, making six in all.

"Would you like to serve me for another year?" asked the wizard; "I will give you six bushels, and that will make twelve in all." The young man refused to serve another year because he was weary and wanted to see new people and new customs, but said that perhaps he would return later.

"Very well," said the wizard, "you will be welcome any time that you may choose to come."

So the young man took his six bushels and started straight for the kingdom about which his beloved had told him. He buried his money in a secret place near the royal palace, and went in to ask whether they would take him into their service. He was given a place as groom and often had the opportunity to ride behind the king. Soon he noticed that the king seemed worried and uneasy, and not very long after that, it happened that one day he came down to the stable while the groom was working there alone. The young man plucked up courage, and begged his majesty's most gracious permission to ask him why he looked so sad and worried.

"It will not do any good to talk with you about that," said the king, "because you cannot help me."

"Your majesty does not know that," replied the groom, "for I know just what is burdening the king's heart, and I also know how the money can be paid."

That was quite another matter, and now the king condescended to talk with the groom, who told him that he could lend him the six bushels of money, but that he would do it only on condition that the king would take him along as his court jester, when he went to the wizard to pay his debt. The groom would play a few tricks, to be sure, for which the king would be responsible, but no harm would come of them. The king agreed with joy to all that his groom demanded, for it was high time for the money to be paid.

When they finally came to the wizard's dwelling, they found that it was not inside of the hill as formerly, but that on top of the eminence there stood a great castle which the groom had never seen before, as the wizard had the power to make it visible or invisible, as he pleased. When they approached the castle, which looked as if it were made of the purest crystal, the young man, in the garb of a jester, ran in advance. He jumped about, threw stones, and broke many of the windows and doors of the castle, and did much damage.

The wizard rushed out in a towering rage and cursed the king for bringing such a wretched fool, and said that he could not compensate him for all the mischief done, let alone pay the debt that he already owed him. Then the jester spoke up and said, "Oh, yes, he is quite able to pay it," and thereupon the king brought forward the six bushels of money. That astonished the wizard because he had not expected it, but he quickly recovered from his surprise and said that the king must now make good the damage caused by his jester. As he was unable to do that, the wizard declared that the king must either answer correctly three questions that he would ask him, or lose his head.

The jester now took his place beside the king and the wizard asked the first question: "Where is my daughter?"

"She is at the bottom of the sea," answered the jester.

"How do you know that?" asked the wizard.

"The little fish saw her there," replied the jester.

"Would you be able to recognize her," the wizard continued.

"Oh, certainly, bring her forth."

Then the wizard caused a large number of maidens to pass before them; but they were not real. Almost the last one was the wizard's daughter, and as she passed the youth she pinched him gently, whereupon he seized her and held her fast and the wizard had to acknowledge that the first question had been answered.

Then he asked, "Where is my heart?"

"It is in a fish," answered the youth.

"Can you recognize this fish?"

"Bring him out," said the jester.

Then a multitude of fish came swimming past them, while his beloved stood beside him. When at last the right one came, she touched the young man, who immediately seized the fish and slit him open with his knife; then he tore out its heart and cut it in two.

At the same moment the wicked wizard fell dead, and all the fetters and charms that he had laid were done away with, and all the wild animals and birds resumed their human forms and scattered. Then the youth and the maiden went into the castle which now belonged to them, and were married, and all the kings who were debtors to the wizard came to the wedding, and elected the young man emperor. And he ruled over them wisely, and lived happily with his dear empress in their beautiful castle, where they are living today, if they are not dead.

The
White Dove

There was once a king and he had two sons. They were daring young fellows and were always thinking up some new piece of recklessness. One day they rowed out to sea all alone in a small boat. At first they had fine weather, but after they had gone some distance a terrible storm arose. The oars were wrenched from their grasp, and the boat rocked like a cockle shell on the great waves, and was thrown about so that the princes could do nothing else but hold fast to the thwarts to keep from being hurled overboard.

Suddenly they met a singular craft; it was a kneading-trough in which sat an old woman. She called to them and said that she could help them safely to land, if they would promise her the son to whom their mother the queen was about to give birth.

"That we cannot do," they both answered, "he does not belong to us, and so we cannot give him."

"Then you may both rot at the bottom of the sea, for aught I care," said the old woman; "I should think that your mother would rather keep the two sons that she has, than one who is not yet born."

Thereupon she rowed away in her kneading-trough, while the storm howled louder than ever, and the princes' little boat gradually filled, and sank lower and lower in the water. Then the princes thought that there might after all be something in what the old woman had told them; so they called out to her and said that she might have what she wanted, namely their unborn brother, if only she would save them from the terrible danger in which they were. In a moment the storm abated, the sea became smooth, and a gentle breeze drove the little boat to the shore near the king's palace.

The two brothers, however, said nothing about their promise, not even when the queen gave birth to her third son, a beautiful child. He was brought up and educated at the court of his father until he was grown, but his brothers had not yet heard from, or seen the witch to whom they had promised him before he was born.

One evening there arose a terrible storm, and the wind howled and shrieked around the palace, and at the same time there was a violent knock at the door of the youngest prince's room. He went to the door, and there stood before him an old woman with a kneading-trough on her back, who said that he must follow her immediately, because his brothers had promised him to her if she would save their lives.

"If you saved my brothers' lives and they promised me to you in return therefor, I will follow you," the young prince replied.

Then they went down to the shore together, and he had to seat himself in the kneading-trough with the witch, who sailed away across the sea with him to her home. Now the prince was in the power of the witch and had to serve her, and the first thing that he had to do was to strip quills.

"Here is a pile of feathers," said the witch, "and you must have them all stripped by the time I return this evening, otherwise I will set you a much harder task."

He began to work and was doing well, when after a time a whirlwind suddenly arose and scattered all the feathers, so that he had to begin his work all over again. But as it was only an hour until dusk, the prince saw that he would be unable to finish his task before the return of the witch. All at once he heard a pecking on the window pane, and a gentle voice said, "Let me in and I will help you." And there sat a white dove at the window, pecking at the pane. The young man opened the window and the dove flew in and began to work at the feathers; and before an hour had passed all the feathers were stripped; the dove flew out of the window and a few minutes afterwards the witch came in.

"Well, well!" exclaimed the witch, "I should not have believed that you could have arranged the feathers so quickly; you must have nimble fingers."

On the following morning, the old woman called the prince and said, "Today I am going to give you something easy to do. Just outside the door lies a pile of logs which I want you to split up into kindling wood. It will not take you long, but you must be sure to have it done before I come back."

The witch gave the prince a hatchet and he began to hew and split vigorously, and at first it seemed as if he were making good progress; but he soon noticed that it was late in the afternoon and the work was not nearly done. Then he was sad, for he knew that it would go hard with him if the wood were not all split by the time the witch returned.

Then the dove came and seating herself on the woodpile, cooed and asked the prince, "Shall I help you?"

"Yes, I thank you very much for helping me yesterday, and for being willing to help me today," said the king's son.

At once the dove set to work and began to split the wood with her beak, and so quickly did she work that the prince could hardly remove the wood that she had split, fast enough.

When the dove had finished she flew to the prince and seated herself on his shoulder; and he thanked her, and stroked her white feathers, and kissed her pretty beak. And as he did so, the dove suddenly disappeared, and in her place stood a beautiful young maiden. She then told him that she was a princess whom the witch had stolen and changed into a dove, but his kiss had given her back her human form. If he would remain faithful to her and make her his wife, she could easily free him as well as herself from the power of the witch.

The prince was charmed by the beauty of the princess, and was only too glad to do anything that she might wish, in order to win her as his wife. Then she said to him, "When the witch returns, ask her to grant you a wish, because you have performed well every task that she has put before you. And when she consents, ask her for the princess whom she is keeping prisoner here, and

who has to fly about in the shape of a white dove. You must, however, first wrap a piece of red silk about my little finger, so that
you may be able to recognize me in no matter what form I may
appear."

The prince quickly wound a piece of red silk thread about the
finger of the princess, and at once she was changed again into a
dove and flew away. Immediately after that the old witch came
in with her kneading-trough on her back.

"Well, I must say, you are quick at your work," she exclaimed
in astonishment.

Then the prince said to her: "As you are so well satisfied with
my work, you will surely be glad to give me a little pleasure, and
give me something that I am very desirous of having."

"Certainly," said the witch, "what is it that you want?"

"I should like to have the princess who is here, and who flies
about in the form of a white dove."

"Oh, nonsense," said the witch, "how did you ever get the idea
into your head that there are princesses here flying about in the
shape of white doves? But if you really must have a princess I
will give you the prettiest one that I have." And the old woman
went and soon returned dragging a little donkey. "Do you want
this one? she is the best that I have."

The prince looked at the little animal sharply and saw the red
silk thread wrapped around one of her hoofs; then he said right
away; "Yes, I like her very much, give her to me."

"But what do you want to do with her?" said the witch.

"I want to ride on her," answered the prince.

"All right," said the witch, but instead of leaving the donkey
she drew her away.

"what are you doing with my donkey," exclaimed the prince,
"she is mine and I want her."

"Very well," said the witch, and came back with a wrinkled,
toothless hag. "Do you want this one?" said the witch, "you cannot have any other."

"I will take her," said the prince, for he had seen the bit of red silk around the finger of the old woman.

Then the witch became mad with fury and stormed and broke everything about her into pieces, so that the fragments flew about the ears of the prince and the princess, who stood there in her own beautiful form.

Then the wedding was held, for the witch had to keep her promise. But first the princess said to her betrothed, "At the wedding banquet you may eat what you want, but you must not drink a drop, else you will forget me." But when the time came the prince had forgotten the princess' injunction, and was about to drink a goblet of wine. His betrothed, however, was on the watch, and pushed his elbow so that all the wine was spilled on the table cloth. Then the witch again flew into a rage and broke everything, as she had done on the previous occasion.

Then the young couple were led to the bridal chamber, and when the door was closed, the princess said, "Now the witch has kept all her promises and henceforth we can expect nothing good from her, so we must at once betake ourselves to flight. I will put two pieces of wood into our bed, which will answer in our stead when the witch speaks to us. You must also take with you the flower pot and the glass of water standing on the window sill, and then we must slip out through the window and go as fast as we can."

This they did and traveled fast through the dark night, for the princess knew all the ways very well, from the days when she had flown about there as a dove.

Toward midnight the witch went to the door of the bridal chamber and called to the two young people, and the pieces of wood answered her, so that she believed the couple were in there. Shortly before daybreak she again went to the door, and the two pieces of wood again answered her, so that she thought that the prince and his wife were there. And with the first ray of sunlight, as she had kept her promises, she could vent all the bitterness of her fury upon them. So the witch burst into the room but found neither the prince nor the princess, but only the two pieces of wood. These she seized and hurled to the ground with such force that they were dashed into splinters.

And when the first sunbeam fell on them, the princess said to the prince, "Look around, do you see anything behind us?"

"Yes," he said, "I see a dark cloud."

"Then throw the flowerpot backward over your head." When he had done this, a dense forest suddenly grew up behind them, and when the witch came to it, she could not pass through it until she had returned home for an axe with which to hew a path through the woods.

Soon after that the princess again said to the prince, "Look around again and see whether there is anything behind us."

"Yes," he replied, "the great black cloud is again behind us."

"Then throw the glass of water backward over your head."

And when he had done it there was a great lake, which the witch could not cross until she had gone home to get her kneading-trough.

In the meantime the fugitives had almost reached the prince's home. They climbed quickly over the garden wall, ran across the castle park and slipped in through an open window. Now the witch was close behind them, so the princess took her stand in the window and blew down upon the old woman; and as she did so, hundreds of white doves flew out of her mouth, and fluttered about the witch's head, so that she could not see where she was going. That made her so insanely furious that she burst into a thousand pieces.

Now great joy reigned in the palace over the return of the young prince and his beautiful bride. And his two elder brothers came, and fell on their knees before him, and begged his pardon. And after his father's death the youngest son inherited the kingdom and his brothers became his faithful subjects.

The Dreams

*T*here was once a peasant whom everybody knew as the "rich Peter Larsen," and he was the richest man in the whole district; but he was wicked, proud and hard-hearted. He had only one child, a daughter, whose name was Karen. In the same region there lived a poor peasant who had an only son, called Hans.

The children had played and gone to school together and loved each other from their earliest childhood. When they were grown, Hans went to the house of the rich Peter Larsen one day and told him that he loved his daughter and that she loved him, and that he had come to ask Larsen whether he would let them marry. That made the rich farmer furious, and he struck Hans a terrible blow, and then said, "Yes, you may have her, but first you must go to the end of the world. Then you may have her when you return!"

"I will try," said Hans, and went home to his mother and told her that he could have Karen if he would go to the end of the world, and said that he had made up his mind to start at once. Then his mother began to weep and begged him not to leave her. But her tears and entreaties were of no avail for Hans was determined to go. So she gave him a knapsack, and put in some food and a few clothes, and Hans started out on his journey.

He went straight before him, for in that way he would have to come to the end of the world. But as long as he had some food in his knapsack Hans would not turn in anywhere, for he wanted to go as fast as he could. At last a day came when there was not a crumb left in his sack, and he had to stop at a large farm to beg for something to eat. The man to whom the farm belonged asked Hans where he was going, and the young man replied, "I must go to the end of the world, for otherwise I cannot win the daughter of the rich Peter Larsen."

"If you are going to the end of the world, I wish you would do something for me. Find out for me why it is that, although I have three beautiful daughters, and am rich enough to give a large dowry with each one, I can find no suitor for them."

"I will do that, if it is in my power," said Hans, and the farmer filled his sack with food, and again Hans went straight before him, as long as he had a piece of bread. When his knapsack was empty the young man had to stop at a large farm for a bite to eat.

"How far are you going?" asked the owner.

"I am going to the end of the world," answered Hans, "for otherwise I cannot win the daughter of the rich Peter Larsen."

"If you are going to the end of the world," said the farmer, "you must do a commission for me; you must find out for me why it is that a tree in my garden has red leaves on one side, and white ones on the other, and has never borne any fruit."

Hans promised to try to learn the answer to this question, and the peasant filled his knapsack with food, and Hans went on until he again had to stop for food. This time he entered a royal palace and told his story to the king himself, who questioned him, and asked him to find out where his daughter was, who had been stolen seven years ago.

"I will see what I can do," said Hans, "and if it is possible I will let you know."

Then he went on with his full knapsack until he came to a forest in the midst of which stood a sentry box, and near it there was an old soldier on guard. He called to Hans and asked him where he was going, and Hans told him where and why, and also asked whether he had much further to go.

"Not very far," said the old man. "You will soon reach a large body of water; that is the Red Sea, and on the other side of it is the castle that stands at the end of the world; but a wicked wizard lives in it."

"I do not care who lives there," said Hans, "but I must and will go there."

"Then you can do me a favor," said the old soldier, "and find out for me when I shall be relieved, for I have been on duty for four hundred years."

Hans promised to do so and hastened on, and soon he was on the shore of the Red Sea. There he saw an old woman who had a little boat in which she carried people across the sea.

"Where do you want to go?" she asked.

"I want to go to the end of the world," answered Hans.

"You'll get there soon enough," said the old woman, "for you will never come back again."

"Oh, yes!" said Hans, "for I must go back home to marry the daughter of the rich Peter Larsen."

"Very well," said the woman, "I will ferry you across, and if you can return you can tell me how much longer I must stay here paddling around in the water. I have been here for seven hundred years."

"I will try to find out for you," said Hans. And the woman took him across the Red Sea to the castle at the end of the world. He knocked at the gate, and a young woman who was a princess came and opened it, for she was the only one at home then. Hans bade her good evening and asked whether he could stay all night.

"No," said the princess, "what do you want here? If you should once enter you would never cross the threshold alive again."

"But I must enter," said Hans, "for otherwise I cannot marry the rich Peter Larsen's daughter Karen."

"Well," said the princess, "the wizard is not at home now, but if he returns and smells the blood of a Christian, he will kill you."

But Hans insisted that he must see the wizard, because, besides wanting to marry Karen, he had been intrusted with many commissions; and then he told the maiden about the information that he had to secure.

When he told the princess about the king who wanted to know where his daughter was, she burst into tears and said that that must certainly be her father.

"Come in," she said, "and I will try to help you. I shall change you into a brush and put you on a table that stands near my bed, and when I say, 'Brush, pay attention,' you must note carefully what is said." The princess changed Hans into a brush, and soon after that the sorcerer came home.

"Hum . . . Hum," he cried, "I smell the blood of a Christian."

"Oh, no, father!" said the princess, "you are mistaken. Today a carrion crow flew over the palace and dropped some human flesh that he had torn from the body of a man drowned in the Red Sea. That is what you smell."

The wizard was satisfied and sat down to his dinner, and soon afterward he and the princess went to bed, as they were both tired.

In a short time she began to snore so loud that the wizard awoke and came to her room. He woke her and asked why she snored so loud.

"Oh I dreamed something."

"What was your dream?"

"I dreamed of a man who had three beautiful daughters whom nobody would marry, although he would give to each a rich dowry. Why is that?" "I know," said the wizard, "but he never will. If he would let one part of the door open inward and the other part open outward, several suitors would come every day."

"Brush pay attention to that," said the princess.

"Why did you say that?" asked the wizard.

"Oh, I was half asleep when I said it," she answered.

Then they went back to sleep again, but presently the princess again wakened the wizard with her snoring, and he asked her what she had dreamed this time.

"I dreamed of a landowner who has a tree in his garden that has white leaves on one side and red ones on the other, and that has never yet borne fruit. How does that happen?"

"If four of his servants dig on one side, and four on the other, he will find a barrel of gold and a barrel of silver."

After a time the same thing happened again, and this time the

princess said that she had dreamed of a king whose only daughter
had been stolen seven years ago.

"You are the princess," screamed the wizard in such a rage
that the poor young woman feared for her life, and for a time was
afraid to ask any more questions.

After having allowed him to sleep in peace for a time, the princess again began to snore, and the wizard came grumbling to find
out what dream was troubling her now.

"I am just as unhappy about my dreams as you are," said she,
"but I really cannot help them. This time I dreamed about an old
soldier who is standing guard in a dense forest, where he has been
for many hundred years. How much longer will he have to stay
there?"

"I know, but he never will. In order to be relieved he must,
when he hears a rushing sound in the air, call out: 'Hear me
Satan, who art flying and hovering in the air! come down and relieve me. I have been standing here for many a year, now thou
shalt stand here in my place for all eternity.' Then I should have
to descend and stand guard in his place."

Once more the wizard was awakened by the snoring of the
princess, who told him that she had dreamed about an old woman
who lived on the shore of the Red Sea and who wanted to know
how much longer she would have to stay there.

"If she could seize a Christian and break his neck, and then suck
three drops of his blood, she could go where she wanted. And now
see that you do not have any more dreams, or I will break your
neck." Thereupon he fell into a deep sleep and snored so that the
whole castle trembled.

The next morning the wizard got up and went away after
breakfast. Then the princess changed Hans into his original form,
gave him his breakfast and told him to go down to the shore of the
Red Sea. She would follow him as soon as the wizard was far
enough away. Then she transformed Hans into a little wheel
which rolled down to the shore, where it remained until the princess came herself and changed it into a human being. Then they

both jumped into the old woman's boat and told her to ferry them across.

"Have you brought me the answer to my question?" she asked.

"When we are across you shall have it," said Hans. And when they reached land and were some distance from the woman, Hans called back to her how she could free herself.

Then he hurried on with the princess until they came to the sentry box in the woods, and there they stopped long enough to tell the old soldier how to free himself from his guard duty. And even as they stood there, they heard a rushing sound in the air—it was the wizard hastening to overtake the fugitives. Then the soldier called out what he had just learned from Hans, and immediately the wicked wizard had to come down and be a sentinel; and there he stands until this day.

After bidding goodbye to the old soldier, Hans and the princess journeyed to the court of the king, her father. Hans took her by the hand and led her to the king, saying, "Here is your daughter who was stolen from you seven years ago."

At first the king would not believe it, but the princess said, "Father, do you not remember that when I was a small child I fell and cut my right hand with a penknife? Here is the scar."

Then the king was so happy that he had found his daughter again, that out of gratitude he offered Hans her hand in marriage and also the half of his kingdom. But Hans thanked him and said that he must go home to marry Peter Larsen's daughter.

Then the king gave him a hogshead of money, and a fine carriage with a coachman and footmen, and Hans continued his journey to the estate of the landowner who had the strange tree in his garden. Hans gave the desired information and immediately eight men were commanded to dig, four on each side of the tree. And there they found a hogshead of gold on one side and a hogshead of silver on the other. The owner was so glad that he gave Hans half of what had been found, and his servants put it on Hans' carriage. The next stop was at the home of the rich farmer who could not find suitors for his three beautiful daughters. Hans told him how he could remedy that difficulty; and the grateful man wanted to give one of his daughters with a rich dowry to the young man, but he thanked him and told him that he was already engaged.

Now Hans went straight to the house of his parents. His fine carriage stopped in front of the door, and he sent one of his servants to inquire whether he could spend the night there. His mother who did not recognize her son, began to weep and said that he was cruel and heartless thus to mock poor people, for it was evident that they could not accommodate a fine lord in their poor cottage. Then Hans jumped out of his carriage and throwing his arms around his mother's neck he cried, "Don't cry, little mother, it is I, your own son Hans." At first she could hardly believe that it was true, but at last she recognized him, and he sat down and told the story of his adventures, and there was great joy in the little cottage.

The next morning Hans drove with his four horses and servants to the farm of the rich Peter Larsen. Karen was in the act of feeding the cattle, but of course she looked up when she heard the horses, and as she saw the splendid equipage drive into the courtyard she was so surprised that she fell over backward with a bundle of hay in her arms. And the rich Peter Larsen also came out and bowed and scraped most politely.

Then said Hans, "Peter Larsen, it is only I, Hans. May I now have your daughter as my wife? I have just returned from the end of the world. And you remember that once you struck me in the face, and said that if I went to the end of the world and came back, I might marry Karen."

So Hans married Karen and now they are living happily on the farm of the rich Peter Larsen with their children.

The
Reward of
Good Deeds

There was once a man who went into the woods to cut some firewood. He went from one tree to another, but they were all too good for his purpose, as they would make good timber if allowed to stand. At last he found a tree which seemed good for nothing; it was gnarled and partly decayed, so he began to hew away at it.

But just as he began to cut, he heard a voice calling to him, "Help me out, my good man." And as he turned he saw a large viper that was caught in a cleft of the tree and could not free itself.

"No, I will not help you," said the man, "for you would harm me."

But the viper said that it would not hurt him, if he would only free it. Then the man put his axe into the cleft under the snake, and so freed it. But hardly was it free, when it coiled itself up, hissed, put out its tongue and prepared to strike him.

"Did I not tell you," said the man, "that you were a rascal who would reward good with evil!"

"Yes," answered the viper, "you may well say that; but so it is in the world, that all good deeds are rewarded with evil."

"That is not true," said the man, "good deeds are rewarded with good."

"You will not find anybody to agree with you there," said the viper. "I know better how it goes in the world."

"Let us inquire about it," said the man.

"Very well," said the viper. So it did not bite him, but went with him through the forest until they came to an old, worn out horse that was grazing. It was lame, and blind in one eye, and had only a few broken teeth in its mouth.

They asked him whether good deeds were rewarded with good, or with evil.

"They are rewarded with evil," said the horse. "For twenty years I have served my master faithfully; I have carried him on my back, and drawn his wagon, and have taken care not to stumble lest he fall. As long as I was young and strong, I had kind treatment; I had a good stall, and plenty of food, and was well curried. But now that I am old and weak, I must work in the treadmill the livelong day; I never have a roof to cover me, and all the food I have is what I get for myself. No, indeed, good deeds are rewarded only with evil."

"There now, you hear," said the viper, "Now I shall bite you."

"Oh, no! wait a moment," said the man, "there comes the fox; let us ask him for his opinion." The fox came up and stopped and looked at them, for he saw that the man was in serious trouble. Then the viper asked the fox whether good deeds were rewarded with evil or with good.

"Say 'with good,' " whispered the man, "and I will give you two fat geese."

Then the fox said, "Good deeds are rewarded with good," and as he said that he jumped on the viper and bit its neck so that it fell to the ground. But as it was dying it insisted, "No, good deeds *are* rewarded with evil; that I have experienced, I, who spared the man's life, who has now cheated me out of mine."

Now the viper was dead and the man was free. Then he said to the fox, "Come home with me and get your geese."

"No, I thank you," said the fox, "I will not go to town, for there the dogs would get me."

"Then wait here until I come with the geese," said the man. He ran home and said to his wife, "Hasten and put two fat geese into a sack, for I have promised them to the fox for his breakfast today."

The woman took a sack and put something into it; but it was not geese she put in, but two fierce dogs.

The man then ran out with the bag to the fox, and said, "Here you have your reward."

"Thank you," said the fox, "then it was not a lie after all, what I said first—that good deeds are rewarded with good." Then taking the bag on his back he ran off into the woods.

"That sack is heavy," said the fox, so he sat down and tore it open with his sharp teeth. But as he did so the two dogs leaped from the bag and fixed their teeth in his throat. There was no escape from them, so he was bitten to death, but not until he had said, "No, what I said first was a lie, after all; good deeds *are* rewarded with evil."